I0583922

STRANGE IS HER LIFE

SCHOOL OF NECESSARY MAGIC™ BOOK SIX

JUDITH BERENS   MARTHA CARR   MICHAEL ANDERLE

L M B P N

DISRUPTIVE IMAGINATION®

Strange Is Her Life (this book) is a work of fiction.

All of the characters, organizations, and events portrayed in this novel are either products of the author's imagination or are used fictitiously. Sometimes both.

Copyright © 2018 Judith Berens, Martha Carr and Michael Anderle
Cover by Fantasy Book Design
Cover copyright © LMBPN Publishing
A Michael Anderle Production

LMBPN Publishing supports the right to free expression and the value of copyright. The purpose of copyright is to encourage writers and artists to produce the creative works that enrich our culture.

The distribution of this book without permission is a theft of the author's intellectual property. If you would like permission to use material from the book (other than for review purposes), please contact support@lmbpn.com. Thank you for your support of the author's rights.

LMBPN Publishing
PMB 196, 2540 South Maryland Pkwy
Las Vegas, NV 89109

First US edition, October 2018

The Oriceran Universe (and what happens within / characters / situations / worlds) are Copyright (c) 2017-18 by Martha Carr and LMBPN Publishing.

STRANGE IS HER LIFE TEAM

Thanks to Early Readers

Debi Sateren
Michael Robbins
Kathleen Fettig
Terry Hicks Bennett
Bep Hvilsted-Koopman

Thanks to the JIT Readers

John Ashmore
Mary Morris
Angel LaVey
Nicole Emens
Misty Roa
Danika Fedeli
Peter Manis
Daniel Weigert
James Caplan

If we've missed anyone, please let us know!

DEDICATIONS

From Martha

To everyone who still believes in magic
and all the possibilities that holds.
To all the readers who make this
entire ride so much fun.
And to my son, Louie and so many wonderful friends who
remind me all the time of what
really matters and how wonderful
life can be in any given moment.

From Michael

To Family, Friends and
Those Who Love
To Read.
May We All Enjoy Grace
To Live The Life We Are
Called.

CHAPTER ONE

The train slid along the tracks. The lights lining the tunnel were a blur outside the windows as the train moved at incredible speeds. The car was well-lit and filled with magicals. Alison could feel their magic on her skin. Power hung in the air, something she had come to love.

She drew magic around her like a warm coat that smelled of home.

The almost three years she had spent at the School of Necessary Magic had taught her where she belonged in this life, and she did not need to fear or question who she was anymore because of what she was, a Drow Princess.

It was a relief. Accepting herself was so much better than living in fear of who she was and where she came from. Although, Alison wasn't all the way there yet. When she thought about her past, and about the man who had fathered her, all she felt was disdain. It was a long step away from hate, but she wasn't ready to forgive him. She knew she would get there eventually.

Being adopted by James Brownstone and having him as her new father was helping her to get there.

Wasn't that all part of growing up a magical?

Alison looked around in awe at the different kind of magicals around her. Special glasses from Shay that helped her see the world had finally arrived. A gnome with a knack for finding magical, one-of-a-kind artifacts had procured them. He never talked about the how or where of it all.

Through them, Alison could see what was real—not just magic, but shapes and colors and people, as long as they were in the frames. Past the confines of the frames, darkness and the colors of magic or different souls still reigned.

Across from Alison's seat, a Light Elf mother played with her daughter. The child laughed as the mother created creatures of light that danced around them. She swatted at the translucent animals, popping them in a swirl of colored light when she caught them. It was a magical version of blowing bubbles. A nearby witch tsked and rolled her eyes at the minor infraction of using magic on the train. The mother pressed her lips together and sat back, letting the swirling lights evaporate.

A pang of sorrow shot through Alison's chest. She missed her mom. Her mom had been killed, hunted down because of her birth father. It wasn't just death from sickness or an accident. Murder was always harder to deal with, and Alison still carried the pain from being forced to live a life without the person who should have been there to give her guidance.

There was Shay Carson, a wonderful person, and more

than just a guardian to Alison, but she would never replace Alison's mother.

A Kilomea walked past, his footsteps making the whole car shudder. A sense of hostility surrounded the beast, and though she could see what he looked like inside the frames, the aura outside it was an angry, churning red. Alison watched as the hairy beast walked between the seats and stepped on a toy that lay nearby. The Light Elf child stopped humming a song to her mother and froze for a moment.

Being able to see beauty was balanced by being able to see destruction.

The child started squealing, the cries slicing through to the bone, and Alison shook her head as if she could shake off the sounds. The Kilomea grunted, just as irritated with the noise. They weren't patient creatures, and they weren't very forgiving, either.

The Kilomea turned around, raising a hand to the child. Alison could see the beast's intentions, could almost feel the sting on the skin before the hand struck.

Alison jumped up. Her instincts took over. She might not have been allowed to use magic on the train—there were rules and breaking them could result in fines or worse—but she didn't need magic. She had learned a lot from her training with Shay, and a well-placed kick in the beast's ribs did what it needed to do to distract him.

He turned his tusks to Alison and grunted again, eyes filled with anger. The red streaks that swirled around him became darker, flashing faster around him, and it felt a lot more like fury to her, now. Yeah, the annoyance was gone, but unfortunately, it had been traded for something worse.

However, if given a choice, Alison would rather be the target of the anger rather than let it focus on an innocent child.

She spun around, blocked a blow from the Kilomea that came down like a falling tree and placed another kick in the Kilomea's chest.

It all happened so fast that no one had time to react. The Kilomea slid along the floor on his back in the direction he was headed, reaching his destination earlier. *You're welcome.*

A willen in a worn, grey suit jacket stepped out of the way of the sliding Kilomea, and Alison saw him pull his hand from the handbag of the wood elf that stood in front of him. The movement had happened almost simultaneously with the aura of surprise and guilt that permeated the air around the willen. Seeing the auras and watching the actions at the same time came with a strange sense of depth that Alison hadn't experienced before. Although filled with color, her life had been very two-dimensional until now.

Everything happened at once—the train slowed, the Kilomea grunted, the train doors slid open, and the willen slipped through them, disappearing into the crowd.

"Out of the way, out of the way," a wizard and a witch muttered as the passengers started to disembark. They pushed against the crowd, swimming upstream with badges in their hands to get to the Kilomea. The law enforcers looked like ordinary magicals with normal clothes, but they had a stern expression on their faces, and Alison knew they didn't play games.

There was so much to see now that Alison had the gift

of sight. And despite the beauty that took her breath away, there was so much negativity, too. It made her head spin trying to process it all.

As soon as she had a chance, she hopped off the train to follow the willen. She didn't know what he'd taken, but it was wrong. The willen looked over his shoulder, and when he saw Alison following, he moved into the crowd and expertly disappeared.

Alison shook her head. She was a good fighter, but she wasn't good enough. She would have to up her game if she ever wanted to follow in James's footsteps.

With nothing else to do, Alison followed the crowds to the crisscross sets of stairs that led toward the surface in every direction and followed them through the enchanted wall and into the Starbucks on Emmet Street.

All the train stations opened in different Starbucks locations. Just as well—coffee made the world go around, not just for humans but for the magicals as well.

Izzie sat at a table, sipping coffee from a paper cup with her name on it. Alison felt her before she saw her. No matter how much the glasses allowed her to see, she would always use her senses before she used her eyes.

She walked to the table and stared.

Looking at her friend through the glasses was a strange sensation. She was used to how Izzie felt—full of light, with dark spots in her soul that Alison had become used to by now. Seeing her in person was fascinating, with her dark hair pulled back in a ponytail and eyes like gems, almost glowing, but not quite. Her pale skin was perfect and smooth, and she looked like a rare doll, unaware of her own beauty. Alison had to stop herself from staring. Beauty was a word that had meant nothing until now.

"Hey," Alison said, dropping into a seat opposite Izzie.

Izzie looked up. She had dark circles beneath her eyes, and her face was serious. She didn't get up to hug Alison.

"What's up?" Alison asked, but she already knew.

"It's getting worse." Izzie sighed. "It's freaking me out. I feel like it's tearing me apart."

Alison took off her glasses for a moment and looked at her friend the way she'd always done. It was hard to gauge where her friend's emotions were at through a sense she was not accustomed to using.

"You finally got your glasses. Are they everything you wanted?" Izzie was doing her best to look excited for her friend.

"They're weird, and amazing and wonderful. Now that I can see so much, I realize I had no idea what to expect. The best part is I can see your face and your beautiful soul."

The truth was, Izzie's soul was riddled with questions and fear, and the uncertainty was causing red and black streaks through her usual light. The black spots seemed to dance around as if they didn't know where they wanted to be anymore. But relief threaded itself through all the other colors. Izzie could finally talk about what was bothering her again.

"They can't be dreams," Izzie asserted, shaking her head. "They're so much like memories that it takes my breath away. It almost hurts, Alison."

Alison slipped her glasses back on and nodded. It wasn't the first time Izzie had said that—the dreams felt like memories more and more.

"The worst part is that the memories I have of my childhood in the children's home are starting to fade," Izzie admitted. "That's not normal. Aside from the school, the orphanage is all I have. I should remember that clearly. But those are the memories that are starting to feel like a dream. Something isn't right, Ali. I don't know what to do."

Alison reached for Izzie's hand and poured a little magic into her touch, warming her skin.

"We'll figure this out," she said. She didn't know how, yet. But they would. "Let's go. We have to catch the jitney to campus."

Izzie nodded and swallowed the last of her coffee, and the two girls stood, leaving Starbucks to head to the School of Necessary Magic.

Mrs. Beasley, the jitney driver, dropped them off at the main entrance to the school. Alison and Izzie both waved at her as they hopped off and started down the long driveway that led to the main building. Alison held her coat closed against the wind; it had been a cold winter, but there was only a dusting of snow on the ground. A couple of students who also returned early were wandering the grounds. It felt good to be back.

An aura with a flurry of colors caught Alison's attention, just as she noticed Jason Parker. The glasses let her see the face that accompanied the aura she had gotten used to. Everyone had told her Jason was attractive. They were right.

He was tall and thin with a wiry, muscular build. High cheekbones gave him a sophisticated air, and his mop of dark hair was stylishly messy. As usual, his confidence preceded him.

He was talking to a younger student, and the hierarchy was apparent. Then again, Jason considered himself above a lot of people.

When Jason noticed Alison, his face lit up, and he waved. He offered her a charming smile that made him even more attractive. Alison's stomach fluttered just a little. To *see* the effect she had on some people—and not just feel it—made her feel a burst of warmth that she hadn't known before the glasses.

But the dark and swirling threads running through his aura held Alison's attention. Despite his almost rainbow essence, something about Jason didn't add up. Even with the warmth she felt, there was uncertainty. Something about Jason made her feel like she was looking at one face and feeling the aura of another person entirely. But that didn't make sense. Maybe she was just not used to seeing faces along with the magic she felt when she had been blind to it all her life.

A ripple of magic next to her turned Alison's attention back to Izzie. She had her eyes squeezed shut. Her face twisted like she was in pain, and symbols were lit up on her arms—symbols Alison had seen before but couldn't interpret. They ran up Izzie's arms and were glowing brightly. It only lasted a moment before it disappeared, but it left behind a lasting sensation that shouted that it hadn't been only imagined.

"Are you okay?" Alison asked when the power died down again and Izzie opened her eyes.

Izzie started to nod but shook her head instead. She wasn't okay, not at all. Every time this happened, it freaked her out. She felt like she was losing control and being out of control with magic she didn't know anymore scared the shit out of her. What if she did something she would regret? What if she hurt someone? She didn't know how she knew, but her magic was dangerous.

"It's happening more often. It's like the magic is getting away from me." She took a deep breath and let it out with a shudder. Even though the magic had faded, she didn't feel any more stable than a moment ago. That had been getting worse, too.

Jason forgot about Alison and Izzie and went back to focusing on the kid in front of him. The young teenager seemed apologetic about the bit of space in the world he occupied. He had shaggy, brown hair and a body that still had a long way to go before he grew into the likes of a man. He wasn't quite the guy Jason would have associated with, but this was business, not pleasure.

"We're being brainwashed," he continued. "The teachers might be magicals, but they're government appointed. We don't know what they're really teaching us, or if it's what we need to know."

"I hear you," the kid said in a voice that sounded either bored or skeptical. He was a freshman and acted like one, still scared of his own shadow. He chewed on his nail while he listened which irritated Jason. It was a bad habit and showed his insecurity. One of the first things Jason had learned from his father was never to give away how you really felt. A poker face could save you. The people on top never showed they were terrified. That was how they stayed on top. But he swallowed his frustrations because he had to get this done.

"All I'm saying is that when the power shifts and the

magic returns to Earth, we'll have to be ready. Didn't the government already start a bounty system? Specialists who hunt down magicals like me and you."

The kid nodded. Jason narrowed his eyes, trying to figure out if what he was saying was getting through at all. The kid gave him nothing to go by. Talk about poker faces. But maybe this wasn't a mask as much as he really didn't know what was going on.

"So, I need you to figure out who else wants to be a part of this. We need more than just you and me, eh? We're good but not that good."

Jason forced a laugh. The kid only joined in half-heartedly. Jason pulled his parka tighter around himself. He wanted to get the hell out of this cold, but inside the building was the last place he wanted to talk about this.

His assignment was simple in theory. He had to build a team to help take down the school from within. He had been working on it during the Christmas break, doing what needed to be done. But now that he was back at school, and the freshman looked scared to get on board, he knew it wasn't going to be that easy in reality. It irritated him. When he only had himself to rely on, Jason could get shit done. It was when he had to get others involved that it got harder.

Still, he had to succeed. He didn't want to let down his dad. Or the others. They didn't take failure well.

"The normies are acting like they want us to learn and grow and be ourselves. But they're stunting us. We don't know what we don't know. I want to change that. Put a stop to this brainwashing."

"Right," the freshman said.

Technically, what Jason was doing wasn't all too far from brainwashing himself. But who was keeping count? All he had to do was this damn job, and he had been given plebes to work with. He wasn't selling it exactly as it was, but if they were buying, then who cared?

Mara Berens, headmistress and something of a grand-mother to all the students, had supplied Alison and Izzie with champagne to celebrate the New Year. She knew they weren't going to go overboard. The two girls were respon-sible. With both having gone through as much as they had —Alison losing her mother and Izzie having to say goodbye to both parents, even if she couldn't remember it —had caused them to grow up fast. No child should be forced into it, but the world was even further from a perfect place these days, and only the strong survived.

When she checked on the girls, she was a little worried. Izzie looked in bad shape, and worse, she knew exactly why.

Mara felt terrible about it. Every time she thought about Izzie and what she'd done to her, the hard rock of guilt in her gut came back, stopping her from eating and sleeping. She had to push the thoughts away just to func-tion normally. It had been so long. But they had asked her to do, even demanded it, and said it was the only way. It had to be done.

After making sure the girls were okay, she walked to her office and retrieved a hand-carved, wooden box from its shelf. It wasn't very large, only a couple of inches long and as wide as it was deep. The old wood had silvered over time. It had been carved out years ago by gnomes who used to protect the ancient tomes that held the secrets to dark magic that no one was allowed to access.

Mara ran her hands over the intricate design, wondering what the gnome who had carved it had tried to say; what story he had wanted to tell.

With an ancient spell that she passed silently over her lips, she unlocked the box and opened it.

Three balls of light lay side by side in the box, nestled in the velvet that lined the inside. The dark spots that had appeared on them had grown, affecting the shapes of the balls now, and they were giving off fumes, too.

It won't be too much longer, now. Her spell was starting to wear off. Mara swallowed hard, her stomach tightening even more with nerves. She felt as though the burden was getting so heavy to bear that she could hardly stand straight beneath the weight. She had done this to protect everyone involved. When she had done it, she hadn't considered she might fail.

Izzie's Jasper Elf energy was too strong for even Izzie to handle. It reached out and searched for the missing pieces to the puzzle without Izzie's permission. Her desire was strong enough, and her intentions were too strong to hold back. Mara could do nothing to stop it, and nothing to save the child from the danger that came with the instability of her magic or the knowledge of her past.

Mara was ashamed that she had not been able to look after Izzie in the way she had promised she would. This magic was as much of a danger to the girl as everything else that would be unleashed on her once the Jasper magic found all the memories.

And this would be *her* fault, not the fault of whoever was after Izzie. Mara gripped the sides of the box. She would be to blame for whatever Izzie's own reckless magic did to her.

If Izzie was suffering like this, how much did her parents suffer?

Mara closed the box carefully and clicked the lock mechanism shut as she said another spell. She wished it were that easy to make the problem go away. After putting it away, she called her daughter Eireka in Austin, Texas. While she waited, she took a shaky breath and cleared her throat to steady her voice. She hoped that she wouldn't sound as panicked as she felt. She didn't want Eireka to panic.

"It's bad," Mara said as soon as her daughter answered, and Eireka didn't have to ask to know what was going on. "If her origins leak out and come to light, all hell will break loose. You have to move her parents. Get the troll to help you."

Mara was disappointed in herself that it had come to this. She had promised she would help. But if her spells failed, then the past three years would be for nothing.

"I'll do what I can," Eireka promised. "If it's the last good thing we do."

The weekend before school started, students poured in from all corners of the world, and the building that had been asleep for the break was teeming with life again. Students arrived in new clothes they had gotten for Christmas, walking with the confidence that only new outfits could bring, and they shared their holiday activities with friends in high-pitched voices, laughter skipping across the frozen campus as they ignored the cold.

Kathleen, Maya and Emma tried to talk the dragon, Dorvu, into frosting the hillside. It was only the first day back, and already they were bored and looking for a distraction. The dragon, eager for attention after he'd been alone for the break, did as he was asked, and the students slid down the hillside on trays they had borrowed from the dining room. Rules were made to be broken.

Mara watched from the window. The students filled the old school building with life, and it made her happy to see the life back on campus and to feel the youthful energy of their magic fill the hallways and rooms. But her happiness at seeing the students again was overshadowed by the nerves and the worry about what was happening with Izzie. Lately, Mara hadn't been able to focus on much without the dreaded truth nipping at her subconscious.

Professor Hudson stood next to her, biting her tongue and trying not to show her frustration. She was an older witch, and she didn't have time to waste beating about the bush. She was here to talk to Mara about what was going on. She had noticed that the older woman was so worked up over something that her mind wandered away from important conversations.

When Mara had finally told her, Hudson had been shocked, then worried as well, but now she was just upset. Mara was clearly worrying more than enough for the two of them, and Hudson was irritated that Mara had been carrying the burden alone for so long.

"You should have told me sooner," she scolded. Mara had told her in depth about Izzie's memories, and about the lurking danger that she would realize who she was, and the wrong people would be alerted. "I could have helped. I'm the spells teacher, for crying out loud, and one of your oldest friends."

Mara shook her head, avoiding eye contact with Hudson. "I couldn't trust anyone with the secret. I gave my word. But I'm asking now, that should count for something."

Professor Hudson sighed and ran a hand over her blonde hair. She was finally going gray, even if no one would ever know it. She was grateful for a simple spell to dye her hair. It was nothing a few magic words couldn't handle.

"The problem is that there are fewer options now. All we can do is prepare for when her magic finally connects and announces to the world that she's here under this roof."

"We'll need Xander's help," Mara said. She hadn't wanted to go there. She had wanted to keep Xander Powell as far away from this whole mess as she could. But these were desperate times, and what she had done until now just wasn't good enough anymore.

"Of course. But he's not going to like it. He'll be upset that you didn't trust him. Exes are like that."

Mara glanced at Professor Hudson when she said it. It was true—their past would make everything harder. Xander wasn't exactly an easy person to get along with, either. Their history was complicated for a reason. But no matter what Xander's opinion was, it didn't change the fact that Mara had done what she thought was right.

———

Horace stood across from the school building with a hat pulled over his red hair and ears against the cold. The weather was finally showing signs of change, but it would still be cold for a while yet. He didn't particularly hate the cold, but he preferred the heat. It was easier to keep cool than to stay warm. His dog was at his side, and together they watched the kids sliding down the hillside.

The students were pulling off dangerous stunts. Ice and dining trays weren't a good combination in any event. But kids would always look for a way to conjure fun out of thin air, and they would often find the most dangerous way to do it. A life on campus with the students had taught him that where there was creativity, there was also absurdity.

Magic was the only reason there were no accidents today. Someone with a nearby wand or a stream of magic at the last minute had saved more than one student.

Usually, magic was the reason there were accidents. But it was great to see the kids again—Horace hated a quiet campus—and he watched, smiling from the sidelines.

The wind changed direction, and Horace frowned, turning his face to the wind and closing his eyes. He licked the tips of two fingers and held them up in the wind.

"A bad wind is coming," he said to the dog. "Aunt Estelle was right. It's time."

CHAPTER TWO

Luke's nails clicked on the wooden dorm floor as he stretched out in wolf form, his paws eating up the distance. Magic rushed through his system alongside the adrenaline, and he felt wild and free, even though he was still in the school building. When he was a wolf, his ears were sharper, his nose picked up scents he couldn't find when he was human, and magic ruffled his fur like the wind.

He was looking for Peter. A group of juniors were headed out to the kemana to shop, and he wanted his buddy with him. When Luke had started at the School of Necessary Magic, he'd been a bit of an outcast because his magic was so different. Many didn't even think of him as a magical but more like a mutant. But it was his third year, and he had made good friends.

When he couldn't find Peter, he shifted back into human form and sighed before he left the building. He joined the others at the back of the building. Kathleen, Aya,

Jennifer, Ethan, Izzie, Alison, Tanner, and Emma were all waiting for him.

"Let Alison lead and show off her new glasses. After you." Ethan swept out his arm, making way for Alison. She smiled and stepped in front of him.

"Ooh, let me try them. What can you see?" Kathleen clapped her hands together and Alison laughed handing them over to her. She slid them on and looked around, widening her eyes. "Nope, nothing. Are you sure they work?"

Alison rolled her eyes and took them back, sliding them up her nose. "I'm very sure."

"Drow magic, gotta love it."

The group walked together to the hidden entrance at the back of the estate and ducked in, moving down the stairs that led into the belly of the Earth, to the kemana that was situated beneath the school grounds. The glowing staircase spiraled down deeper and deeper. The magical energy made the whole place light up for Alison, who could see all the magic at the hub that fed the school with as much power as it would ever need.

As soon as they reached the archway that announced they had reached Ruby Falls, the bustling city stretched out before them. The giant crystal glowed in the center surrounded by shops in the main circle. The smell of food wafted through the air, making the students hungry for not just the food from the Oriceran, but for a taste of the magic that they weren't allowed to practice above ground.

The neighborhood stretched out on all sides, and the kemana was bursting with magicals who lived there or were visiting for a chance to relax and be themselves. No one had to conform to Earth's societal norms down here where being weird was normal.

The teenagers headed off to various shops, run by different beings. Alison breathed in, tasting the magic in the air, holding it in her lungs before she let it out again. With her glasses on, she could see the kemana for the first time, and it was beautiful. It was like they were at the heart of a rainbow, with jewel-like colors everywhere. There was more color and more power all around her than anything she'd ever felt—or seen—on Earth, and when she was down here, she could never shake the feeling that she was at home.

She passed a stall that was run by Wood Elves. She recognized their magic but saw their faces for the first time. The double iris was strange, and squares of their skin flipped back and forth, shingles that reflected light, allowing them to blend into the background. Watching them was fascinating, like an illusion made real.

When they looked at her, their expressions changed, and their pupils shifted to one another and back to her.

What are you staring at? Never seen a Drow before?

Their expressions were clear, but they weren't going to be rude and chase away a potential customer. Alison knew she was making it awkward by staring right back at them, but there was so much to take in.

Alison looked around and committed to memory the sight of the pixies, gnomes, faeries, and more. The visual input was almost too much for her to handle. She had relied on her magic and senses, hearing and touch and taste, for so long without ever relying on what she might see. There was almost too much to look at, and Alison decided she would have to come back again to really take it all in without feeling like she was going to miss something.

Izzie walked around the market. She had come down with the group although she had to put on a smile to hide her mood because being alone was worse. Somehow, she had split off from the group anyway and wandered in between the stalls where magicals sold and bartered their wares.

She didn't see anything for sale. Her attention was turned inward, to her magic. Her power was ramped up. The closer she stepped to the crystal, the worse it got. It was like a beast lying in wait, threatening to break free and do something terrible at any moment. And she wouldn't be able to stop it, or predict it, or protect anyone from it.

Her skin shivered with the magic that coursed through her body like an electric current. Her skin glowed every now and then, making her feel like she was the center of attention when she didn't want to be. Everyone who walked by her glanced in her direction at least once as if something was wrong with her. Nothing was as troubling as a double take when the first look already made her feel insecure as hell.

An image flashed before her eyes, drawing her away from the surroundings again—the shadows of a man and a woman fighting alongside her. The bond between them was strong, and the magic was like a smell she could not quite place. A lot of Izzie's memories were like that, lately. They seemed familiar. Izzie reached out her hand to touch the figures as the image disappeared, and she realized she was still in the middle of the marketplace, standing with her hand outstretched. A Light Elf stood in front of her, blinking in surprise. She had nearly pushed a hand into his face.

"Sorry," Izzie mumbled and hurried away, feeling like an idiot.

Other magicals had started walking around her, giving her a wide berth as if they wanted to avoid her. Maybe they had seen her trying to touch things that were not real. Maybe she looked crazy. *Maybe I am crazy*. Izzie looked around and swallowed, her throat feeling tight. The power was so strong inside her that Izzie feared it would tear her apart, spilling out of her like a waterfall of light.

As Izzie moved along, caught up in the power that coursed through her, a wizard followed—not too closely, or the magic would burn him. He was shrouded in a dark cloak and kept to himself to avoid drawing attention. Anywhere with enough light magic had beings that would point out that he was out of place and bring scrutiny. It was a risk following the magical female through the kemana when he should have focused on himself and keeping his cover in place. But he needed to know for sure if what he saw, what he felt, was correct—if this was indeed *her*.

The others in the group enjoyed themselves, moving from store to store picking up different things to see what they would do. In the kemana, there was so much to see and to try. The stores had everything from spelled objects that could help with different problems, trinkets that could be exactly what the receiver wanted them to be, to potions that could do all kinds of magic for the consumer. An apothecary had a wall filled with small, glass bottles from floor to ceiling with different sized tags hung on each one, labeled in a dark script. Heal a cold, change the color of their hair, stop their mate's snoring, and there was even a love potion or two.

Alison, Kathleen, Ethan, and Emma wandered into a shop that was filled with small crystals of different colors set in necklaces, earrings or brooches. They lent the wearer different abilities. Alison studied a necklace that allowed the wearer to see the magic that clung to individuals. It was bizarre—here she was with that ability as an everyday thing. Her sight with the aid of the glasses was the gift. There were others who took seeing for granted and wanted to sense auras, something that was normal to her. Everyone was different, and it was strange how everyone wanted exactly what they couldn't have.

"Come on, Ethan," Kathleen said, standing on the other side of the store. Her red hair hung in a braid down her back. Ethan turned a brooch over and over in his hand, trying to figure out if it was worth the price.

"What?" he asked.

"That magic is far too weak for the likes of you. A brooch to make you cool? It won't work. Besides, wearing a brooch is weird for a guy."

"Hey, I was just looking," Ethan said defensively. "I know I'm cool."

"Is that right?" Kathleen grinned. "So, be *cool* and do a spell. We can do whatever we want down here. There aren't the same rules about magic."

On Earth, there were rules about when the magical students were allowed to practice, and where. School grounds, usually during a class while under the watchful eye of a professor, and not a lot more than that. It was a different story in the kemanas, where magic was all that mattered, and where it was the very life force that drove them.

"We're in a crystal shop," Emma pointed out. "Everything can break here, and Ethan doesn't have a great track record when it comes to controlling himself."

"Hey, I'm not a child anymore. I know what I'm doing," Ethan retorted. He wasn't going to back down. He was going to prove he was as cool as the rest of them—even if he slipped up now and then. Magicals could be clumsy, too; it said nothing about his ability. "Look." He took out his wand and twirled it in the air.

"You break; you buy," the faerie who manned the shop announced. She was tall and slender with silver hair that hung to her thighs and wings like spun sugar. Her face was pinched. She was nervous about the students in her shop, and what they would break. They didn't look like they could afford to break anything.

"I'll be fine," Ethan called, looking over his shoulder. He shook his arms, loosening his shoulders and tilting his head side to side as if he was going to run a race.

"Be careful, Ethan," Alison said. "Why don't we leave the shop before you do something?"

Ethan rolled his eyes. "I'll be fine. Challenge accepted."

As soon as he shifted his attention away from his wand, a thin stream of magic slipped out and shot toward a display.

"Or... not. Shit," he muttered and tried to catch it again.

It was a disaster waiting to happen. None of them could afford even part of the crystal display.

"Should have thought about that."

"Too late now," said Emma, sucking in a breath, waiting for the inevitable tinkling of broken glass.

He always tried his best, but it was true—he was clumsy with his magic and lacked control.

What a way to be forced to admit to it.

Alison jumped forward, shoving her hands toward the magic, summoning her Drow power and releasing it. It hummed inside of her like a second heart beating, a power that had been dormant before she had realized who she was. The school had been teaching her how to rein her magic in—she was so powerful that she didn't need to learn to reach out. Control was everything, here. But she had more control than Ethan, and under pressure, she was even better than when she had to think about it.

She caught the stream of magic before it crashed into the display and smothered it until it burned out.

"Don't screw around in the shops," she admonished tightly. Ethan was clever at pranks, but his magic often got the better of him. His scruffy appearance mimicked what his magic was like—all over the place.

He rubbed the back of his neck, tucking away his wand with a sheepish grin. He felt like an idiot and probably looked like one, too. "Thanks, Ali."

Kathleen laughed out loud. "That was fun."

Ethan shot Kathleen a dirty look. She had encouraged him to do this. But even though he was pissed off—at himself and at her—he couldn't blame her for this. She had been the one to suggest it, and Kathleen was known to push people into things, but he had still made that choice himself. It was a matter of owning up to his mistakes.

Thankfully, there was no shattered merchandise.

"Until you had to pay for it," Emma said, voicing his thoughts. She looped her hand through Kathleen's arm. "Let's get out of here."

The faerie watched, relieved, as the teenagers left the shop without anything broken in their wake.

"Where to?" Kathleen asked. "Ali?"

Alison shrugged. "I'd like to buy a book or two."

She loved reading. She couldn't read with her glasses on because she had only learned to read braille. There were still spells that turned normal print in books into braille for her. All the books in the library had been spelled so that she could read them, and she loved immersing herself in worlds other than her own. After her mother had died and her father—the scheming son of a bitch—had been taken away, other worlds in books of old were what had kept Alison distracted long enough that her subconscious could work through the worst of the issues, so she wouldn't explode in a rage.

"We should buy Aya a doll," Kathleen suggested. "Something scary that we can use to prank the boys with, make it float around their dorm room."

"Funny," Ethan said. They had enough troubles with the damn squirrel that just wouldn't leave them alone. The doll would only add to it, and he didn't feel like having the crap scared out of him in the middle of the night.

"Oh, you're a boy," Kathleen said. "I forgot."

Ethan rolled his eyes and bumped into Luke, who was coming around the corner. The magicals around them eyed Luke. He was a shifter, and most people didn't consider him a real magical, but there was nothing he could do about who he was, and they couldn't ban him from the kemana. Shifters had been living in kemanas for generations.

Besides, over the course of the past semesters, his friends had gotten used to who he was, and they knew he was a great guy. It was just down here in the kemana the differences between them were more obvious. His eyes glowed, and he could feel the desire to shift just beneath the surface.

It was only when they were down here that some students could get a little nervous about what Luke was capable of doing.

"I was in dire need of male backup," Ethan said, high-fiving Luke and sending sparks flying to make it more impressive.

"If Peter were here, there'd be three of us," Luke mused, shaking the magic off his hand.

"Where is he?" Ethan asked.

"I couldn't find him," Luke shrugged.

Kathleen laughed again. "You boys seemed to have lost a musketeer."

They moved along, Ethan and Luke pairing up and trailing behind, chatting and laughing. Ethan was glad to be away from Kathleen and to have Luke with him. Kathleen could be a handful sometimes, and he wasn't always in a forgiving mood. But down here, everyone's magic was a little more intense, and everyone felt a little bigger and a little braver than when they were further away from the crystal that charged them like a giant battery.

The teenagers passed a new shop that mixed magic with technology. Luke and Ethan were drawn in immediately, and the rest followed. They were both interested in blending the real with the fantastical, and magic combined with human invention was the best of both worlds. They worked their way through the shops.

"Peter would love this shop," Luke admitted. "It has everything he likes."

"So, come here again with him next time," Kathleen said. Alison sighed. Kathleen was particularly chatty today, nudging whenever she could.

"A GPS that locates spells," Ethan murmured. He focused on the trinket he'd found.

"You should get that for Peter," Kathleen piped up.

Ethan ignored her, irritated. Responding would only make it worse. He picked up a watch and studied the face, which seemed to show things other than time.

"I'm hungry," Emma complained.

"Yeah, me too," Kathleen agreed. Alison nodded as well. They had been wandering around for a good two hours, and they were all hungry.

"Fine." Luke sighed, putting back the GPS he'd been looking at. "There's nothing worse than a hungry elf. Let's get food. Where did Izzie go?"

They left the shop and walked to the food court together. Luke found Izzie and slipped his arm around her waist, walking with her to join the others. They passed different magicals, and it was different than being on Earth —down here, there were no humans allowed—no one besides Horace, that is. He was one of the rare humans that even knew of the existence of kemanas.

The magicals that passed them all practiced magic in the open without looking around to see who might be watching, not guarded or worried at being caught. They were proud of who they were. It encouraged the students to do the same. Still, Izzie was doing her best to reign in the occasional flash of energy.

After walking into a restaurant and finding a table, the group sat down and talked and laughed.

Through her new glasses, Alison could see the faces, and how they changed when the auras changed. She could see the events that caused them. It was a new experience, and she thoroughly enjoyed herself.

They ate together, throwing spells around, causing light-hearted trouble that they could contain. Even Ethan was keeping a lid on it this time, careful not to do something that would get away from him the way it had inside the store. "I hear you almost cost us our first born back in the store," said Luke. "That sounded intense." He gave Ethan a good-natured pat on his back, getting a wide grin from him.

"I try... I try..."

When they were done eating, they stood and cleared their table with magic, evaporating the garbage rather than looking for a bin.

"Magic has its perks," admitted Izzie, managing a smile.

"Let's find the rest of the gang and head back to the school," Ethan said. "I have one last surprise before school starts."

When they arrived at the school, Ethan led them around the building to the garages and opened the last two wooden doors.

"Ta-da!" he exclaimed proudly. Ethan was clumsy with his magic, but he was a whiz with his hands, and he was proud of himself. The others walked into the garage, whistling and gaping.

It was the car they had worked on together in class then nearly crashed. A 1976 Chevette hatchback. It had been broken-down and rusted, but with a bit of magic and paint, it was good as new in a pale metallic blue. It was the color of the sky if the sky could be bottled.

"Are we allowed to be here?" Alison asked. She had been in cars many times and felt the metal under her hands, but she stared at the car, drinking in the color. She had seen auras and magic this color, but it was different in real life. The car was beautiful to look at with the light reflecting off the paint.

"Never even been able to imagine one before," she said, taking in a short breath.

"Of course," Ethan said. "Professor Heineken said we could use it. I swear. I even have my shiny new license I got over break. Let's try it out and we can head into town for dinner tonight. It will be cool."

Everyone agreed, even Izzie, who had started to open up again once they were back at school and away from the crystal that drew her magic out even stronger.

Going to the kemana had made her feel more like an outcast because of her magic. It was supposed to make her the same as the rest. *They all have control...* And she didn't. *I feel like a loser who can't keep it together.* It was making her nervous and irritated. And different. Over the past few years, she had finally started fitting in, and found friends—

29

people she could refer to as a family. But she was starting to feel more and more lost again.

Like she belonged somewhere else.

"I'm going to go find Peter," Luke blurted. "I don't want to go without him."

"Let him do his own thing if that's what he wants," Ethan said. "Come on. This is too good. You can't pass it up."

Luke hesitated. He was worried about Peter. Usually, the three of them were attached at the hip, but he hadn't seen his friend since they had returned to campus, and that was weird.

He knew he was there, though. His things were unpacked in his nightstand and dresser. He was there but occupied with something else. Luke knew something had been on his friend's mind for a while now, but Peter didn't talk about much lately.

"Fine," he finally said. "Let's do it."

The students drove through the main gate with the icy wind whipping the girls' hair into a mess through the open windows. Luke and Ethan were up front. Kathleen, Izzie, Alison, and Emma were in the back. The others had decided to stay home.

"It's a good thing it's just us," Kathleen said, shifting under Alison, who sat on her lap. "There's no way we would have squashed more than four of us back here."

The girls laughed. Alison tried not to put her full weight

on her friend. The car was filled to the brim with magic, and it was like a soup of power as they drove to downtown Charlottesville. The street was lined with shops that were lit up, and people were everywhere. The crowds were beautiful, with faces that were all unique and so many more colors than Alison saw when she only looked at auras.

They parked at the mall and piled out of the car, stretching their legs. Ethan ran his hand along the car's hood.

"Smooth ride," he said.

"Yeah, you did good," Luke agreed, and Ethan beamed.

"This is great," Kathleen exclaimed, her cheeks flushed. She let out a ripple of magic. It traveled across the parking lot, setting off two different car alarms.

"Not here," Alison warned. "We have to be careful."

Kathleen rolled her eyes and flicked her red hair over her shoulder.

"I get it," she said and stopped.

They walked around the sidewalks at the Charlottesville mall, looking for a restaurant. Alison looked around, again in awe of all the colors and shop displays. These were the things she'd missed when she hadn't been able to see colors and light and shapes. Mannequins in shop windows showed clothes of the latest fashions, and the colors were all bright, the fabrics decorated with beautiful prints.

"We should come and try these on sometime," Izzie stated when she saw Alison looking.

Alison nodded, agreeing. They moved from one shop to the next, and Alison took it all in. Izzie smiled, watching her friend as they moved along, enjoying her reactions. She felt herself starting to relax a little.

Before they arrived at the restaurant, they bumped into a group of normie teenagers. Alison saw their auras, the different shimmers of color. There was a tension running through them.

Alison and her friends knew them. Once upon a time, during a class outing when they'd had to learn to blend in, they had made friends. Now, it was awkward. Luke stepped up and held out his hand.

"It's good to see you again," he said.

The humans looked at each other and didn't accept the handshake. The world had mixed feelings about magicals, and a new type of discrimination had hatched recently. Bad press had made things difficult, and no one knew where they stood anymore.

Humans didn't always get along with magicals, and the magic was too foreign for them not to care in some way or another about their safety and what it might mean if they accepted the magicals.

"It's a nice night," one of them said tightly, making small talk when they didn't know what else to say. Being polite was a good start.

Everyone nodded and agreed. Alison focused on what she felt, not what she saw. The magicals were all giving off vibes of disappointment and awkwardness. She couldn't tell what the humans felt, but their faces told her they didn't know what to do, either.

"Let's go. We'll lose our reservation," Ethan said. He hadn't made a reservation, but he wanted to get away from the normies that looked at them like they were creatures that belonged in a zoo. "Sorry, excuse us."

The magicals pushed past the humans, going on their way. It looked almost like they were relieved to escape and wanted to get away as fast as they could.

"It was good seeing you," one of the teenagers said to Luke. He held out his hand, an idea that was almost too late. Luke could have let it go the way they had done to him, but he turned back and shook the young man's hand. Magicals and humans can be on the same side.

His animal instinct picked up on the normie's fear, triggering his anger. *Why do humans fear me on sight?* But there was nothing to be done. They all feared what they didn't know, and magic had been hidden away for so long, it was understandable.

He turned and followed the others to the restaurant, knowing at least that he had done the right thing.

"Magicals have to adapt so quickly," said Ethan.

"It's unfair that the humans weren't forced to do the same," complained Kathleen, for once on the same side with Ethan.

"It'll take time for everyone to get on board with the way things are changing," said Izzie.

"Everything takes time, and this will, too," Alison chimed in, happy to see Izzie participating in the group. Maybe there were better days ahead.

CHAPTER THREE

Peter sat on the city bus, watching the scenery go by as it made its way to the center of Charlottesville. He was sitting just behind the bus driver, an older man in a neat green uniform with a paunch that rested right on the steering wheel. He had a calm demeanor interrupted by the occasional slurp of the candy in his mouth.

"Whatcha doin' out so late kid, and on your own? Where you supposed to be?" He smacked his lips together as he talked, glancing up in the rear-view mirror.

"I'm on my school newspaper and I'm following a lead. I take it very seriously. Been doing it for two semesters now. Think I may have a talent for it."

"Was it necessary to prove your talent tonight?" The driver raised an eyebrow, smacking his lips.

"A good story doesn't wait. Journalism is no joke. Sure, it's just a school newspaper, but I have to start somewhere, right?"

"I hear ya' kid. Good for you. That's how you get somewhere in this life. A hot lead… make sure it don't take you straight into some kind of fire."

"No, sir. I'll be careful." He settled back in his seat, pressing his lips together.

Peter left out that the lead was about dark magic. There were things out there the students deserved to know, and he was on it. The magicals were excluded from a lot in the human world, which he couldn't do anything about. But they deserved to know what was happening.

Knowledge was its own kind of power.

He had long ago decided that just because they were kids, it didn't mean that the world was too scary for them. They were learning how to hone their magic skills. They were being taught how to handle the magic and stand together when the gates of Oriceran finally opened again.

"Okay, kid. I think this is your stop, right? Go save the world but be back on the bus by ten before we shut down for the night. Even heroes need their rest."

The driver opened the door, and Peter gave him a wave and stepped off, looking around at his surroundings.

"I can do this," he muttered to himself. He dug his hands into his pockets as he walked to keep them warm, talking to himself to keep up his courage. "We should have been better prepared to fight. How could we be left not knowing exactly what we're facing?"

"Hey, kid! Watch where you're going!" Peter looked up in time to see the angry face of a tall man; his hat knocked to the ground. Peter had jostled him while lost in thought.

"Sorry about that," he said quickly, picking the fedora up off the icy ground. "Here you go," he stammered, handing over the hat.

The man took it out of Peter's hands and settled it on his head. The woman next to him teetered on high heels, grasping the man's arm as she tsked. "Probably on his phone. Kids these days."

Something jabbed Peter's wrist, and he realized almost too late that his wand was poking out of his sleeve. He pushed it back in and looked up to see if anyone had noticed, but they were already picking their way carefully across the ice, their backs to him.

His phone buzzed, and he took it out of his pocket. It was Luke again, trying to find him. "Sorry, brother, not tonight." He was serious about finding out who had been in the woods talking about taking down the school. "There are real boogeymen in the world. My own kind, and I know they're nothing to mess around with." He pocketed his phone without answering. Luke would only try to talk him out of his mission.

He checked his notes. The wizards were looking for a particular female student. But he still didn't know who. He tapped his pen against the paper, even as he made his way down the sidewalk.

A plan to break in past the glamours and spells around the school, but again, Peter had no idea how they would pull it off. "Not much of an ace journalist," he muttered.

What if they succeed? What if something goes wrong? That thought had driven him out into the night to pursue a hunch. He'd gotten a tip out of a pixie named Dorothy who worked in the kitchen at the school. Peter bribed her with a box of cronuts and the promise of a box a week for a month. Pixies were known for their sweet tooth.

Dorothy had a good-for-nothing cousin she was always

complaining about to anyone who would listen. She had told him that some dark wizards from out of town were planting themselves in a back booth of a particular bar most nights.

"But, you don't want to go near trash like that, honey. That's what happened to my cousin, let me tell you," she had said, getting ready to wind herself up into another long story. Peter had pushed the box of cronuts closer to her, a winning distraction and gotten out of the kitchen in time to catch the bus.

Now, here he was, looking for a story.

It was a moonless night, and the street was dark in between each decorative streetlight. He got goosebumps and swallowed hard. Being so worried was just silly. He pushed away the nerves. *I'm doing the right thing.*

He stopped and looked up at the sign. *Gotham City.*

"Someone has a sense of humor." Inside weren't human locals—they were low-life, good-for-nothing magicals. He was just a teenage reporter with a live, oak wand way out of his league and even further out of his comfort zone. "Well, only one way to find out who was in the woods that night and what they wanted."

He pushed open the glass door, walked into the bar and sat down at a small, round table near the front, squaring his shoulders and willing himself to look older. Magicals came in all shapes and sizes. He could be older but look like shaving was still in his future, right?

He glanced around, feeling eyes on him, but he avoided making eye contact with anyone. Maybe if he didn't make eye contact, they wouldn't think twice about him, and they wouldn't ask questions.

The last thing Peter needed was for an adult to question him about why he was there.

"What'll you have?" A tall, reedy waiter hunched over him, impatiently tapping his foot.

"Uh, cheesy fries. You got cheesy fries?"

The waiter smirked and rolled his eyes. "Seriously? You want that; go crawl over to the diner. Let me make this easier for you. What are you drinking?"

"A beer," he squeaked, trying to sound confident.

"We have a dozen different kinds. Name one."

"You pick."

The waiter eyed him suspiciously. "You got money? I mean real money. Not that funny stuff they use underground."

Peter pulled out a wad of bills and showed them to the waiter, shoving them back in his pocket.

"Fair enough, I'll choose for you," he said as he walked away, his hunched shoulders helping his head lead the way.

Peter played with the candle in the center of the table, doing his best to listen to the conversations around him. The locals sat in small groups, drinking and talking about betting on a game of Louper, or how much they hated working with a willen. "Necessary evil, my friend. Best little thieves around."

"Just have to make sure they don't steal you blind."

"True that. Some is okay, just the price of doing business. Too much, make willen stew."

The waiter brought back the beer and set it down on the table, sloshing a little. "That'll be five dollars, up front." He held out his hand, tapping his foot again. Peter started to question the price but thought better of it and handed over the five-dollar bill. "This don't include a tip," said the waiter, closing his fist around the money, and walking away with his elbows working out by his sides.

Peter took a sip and nearly spit it back out again. "Holy shit!" The group at a nearby table looked at him, a few of them laughing. A gnome raised a glass and gave him a wink. He tried another sip and swallowed hard. "Why do people pay for this?" he muttered under his breath.

He looked around and realized no one cared he was there. He felt himself relax a little, and his breathing evened out.

Time to get to work. He glanced around at other tables, careful not to look like he was staring. There were a few wizards, but only one of them looked vaguely familiar.

A wizard was hunched over his glass at the bar; his legs manspread the width of two seats. *Was he there that night? Can't be sure.* Peter had caught only a glimpse, and even then, it had been very dark. He tried to imagine the wizard's face from that night. *No, nothing. What am I doing here?*

The wizard leaned closer to the magical next to him, talking animatedly about something.

Peter leaned to the side in his chair, his beer in his hand and tried to catch some of the conversation. Maybe, if he could pick up something worth his while, he would know if it was him or not.

The wizard looked up at him, dark eyes burning a hole in Peter's soul.

Peter looked right back at him and knew. *It's him. He's one of them.*

The wizard sneered, curling his lip and saying something, but Peter wasn't going to stick around to find out what. He knew when he was in trouble, and he wanted to get out of there before the trouble had a chance to catch up with him.

He jumped out of his chair and ran for the door.

Shouts and cries rose up behind him as he left the bar, knocking over a patron's drink, angering a Kilomea.

"This is why you get 'em to pay up front," yelled the waiter above the din.

Peter got to the door and burst out onto the sidewalk, turning in a direction—any would do—and ran down the street. He blindly turned another corner. Anything to get out of sight.

Dead end.

Shit.

When he spun around, the wizard walked into the alley. He had a wicked grin on his face and black eyes that glowed in the night. He moved slowly, like a predator closing in on his prey.

"It's rude to listen in on other people's conversations, boy," the wizard said, in a voice that caused Peter to shiver. "Didn't your mommy teach you that? Do I know your mommy?"

He kept walking, closing the distance between them. Peter stepped back, stumbling over a black plastic bag full of trash, but catching himself in time. He fumbled for his wand.

"You're gonna need something to get out of this alley," sneered the wizard.

Peter had to do something to stop the attack. "I know a few spells. Not exactly trained in hand to hand or even magical combat, but I get good grades." He pulled out his wand and held it up in front of himself.

"Do you, now?" The wizard let out a sinister chuckle. He smiled, waiting to see what Peter could do. It was his entertainment for the night.

The wizard came closer still, daring Peter to do something. Peter mumbled a spell, rushing through it. The words tumbled weakly out of his mouth, and he mispronounced the last word. The spell wasn't nearly as strong as it should have been. "Professor Powell would be very disappointed right now," he whispered.

Blue flames shot out from his wand and ran up the wizard's arms. The wizard brushed it off just as quickly. Peter had hoped that he would try a little harder to put it out. "Not even a stop, drop, and roll?" he squeaked out. He tried again, and this time the wizard caught the flame and bent it into a spear, throwing it into the ground where it was absorbed in a flash.

"Great, now he's even showing off. It's like a deadly Vegas show."

The wizard smiled and shrugged. "Kid, you amuse me but not for much longer."

The wizard pulled out his wand and held it out for Peter to admire. "See kid? Something like this." He cleared his throat, taking his time and cast a spell, working his wand like a baton in front of an orchestra. Thin streams of magic curled out of his wand, seeking out something.

The streaks were black and snaked around the wizard like a caress before it came toward Peter. It was terrifying. Darkness swam through the air and wrapped itself around Peter's throat, burrowing into his chest and making him feel like every breath was on fire. He coughed and fell to his knees. He felt like he was being sliced up from the inside like the darkness was a thousand knives. He doubled over, trying to get the pain and the strange sensation that he was being consumed by the darkness to stop.

"If you want to play with the big boys, better bring a big wand," the wizard said, giving him a wink. His voice sounded muffled to Peter. He cast another spell, the magic shoving Peter to the ground. He lay flat on his back looking up at the few stars he could see, coughing and trying to remember how to breathe again.

The wizard walked to Peter and crouched next to him. His face was filled with malice. His smile was sinister. Peter looked up at him and those dark eyes that looked all wrong because wizard's eyes shouldn't glow.

"You think you can stop this? I guess it's cute you think you can try. But we're still coming." He rocked on his heels. "We're sick of being second-class citizens, hiding behind the normies, watching your lot being trained by them. It's pathetic, all the magical sheep in their flock. Think you fingered me? No matter. Clock's ticking, boy. Tell who you want."

Peter gasped for air, trying to find his voice. He wanted to know what they wanted. Even through the pain and his struggle for air, he knew he was onto something big, and he wanted to know because if he didn't find out, then no one would. He gasped for air like a fish out of water, and the wizard laughed, a nasty, wheezy sound void of mercy.

The wizard stood and kicked Peter in the ribs. A sharp pain shot through his chest, and it was as if the darkness inside of him spread, a poison that sucked him temporarily dry of his own magic.

"You're a tough one. I'll give you that." The wizard nodded, watching Peter struggle, trying to push himself up. "Pity. Should have stayed in school." He laughed at his own joke before he lifted his leg and brought a boot down on Peter's face. Maybe the blow would have been tolerable if it had been just a boot. It would have hurt like a bitch, but it would have been nothing more than another hit.

But the wizard had loaded that hit with magic, and when he kicked Peter in the face, Peter felt himself falling, falling, falling into the abyss.

Henry and Wyatt found Peter. Someone at school finally decided he was missing. It had taken a small locater spell to find him—they had learned it last year, and Wyatt was hella grateful he'd paid attention in class instead of screwing around again. He was taking his studies seriously this year.

When they finally reached Peter, he was in a bad way in an alley. They ran to him, terrified he was dead. But at least it wasn't that bad. Nothing could be that bad.

"We can't move him like this," Henry said, pressing his fingers against Peter's neck. "What do we do in a situation like this? Don't remember being taught first-aid for combat."

"Hell, I don't know. We have some magic at our disposal, but dragging a limp body through town is going to draw attention." Wyatt looked at the marks along

Peter's neck. "This was done by dark magic, damn," he said, looking nervously around. "If there's one dark wizard in town, there will be more. Their kind travel in packs."

"What else are we supposed to do? We have to get him out of here." Henry was on his knees, still trying to locate Peter's pulse. He felt the pulses of dark magic pounding right next to Peter's heartbeat. The magic was strong, and his pulse was weak.

"There's not much time. We have to open a portal, get him straight to the infirmary."

Wyatt bent over to get a better look and straightened up, looking down the empty alley. "Opening portals is against all kinds of rules. That could get us expelled in our senior year."

Henry rolled his eyes. "Letting Peter die is not an option. We can't get him back any other way without the normies noticing. The longer we take, the harder this spell will be to reverse."

"You don't have to be a dick about it. Okay, okay, I'll do it."

Wyatt shouted, *"Portalus perdus!"*

The portal opened into the front hall of the school.

"You couldn't just open one right at the infirmary?"

"I'm nervous. Performance anxiety. I undershot the mark."

Together, they pulled Peter up, each looping an arm around their necks, dragging the limp body through the opening.

Sparks sprayed across the alley as the portal closed. Henry lifted Peter into his arms and ran with him as fast as he could through the halls toward the infirmary, Peter's head bouncing against his shoulder.

"Hey! Hey, help!" yelled Wyatt, remembering he had a wand and waving it to send out an alarm ahead of them. The school nurse came rushing out to take over followed closely by Professor Hudson in her robe, running from her cottage behind the main building.

"Dark magic," said the nurse, shaking her head. "Carry the boy in here."

Professor Hudson began whispering a spell while Professor Fowler brought a case of jars filled with potions.

She grunted, bearing down to open the tight lid and letting out a vaporous orange gas. Henry and Wyatt covered their noses. The smell made it hard to breathe, making their eyes water from the stench.

"You should leave," Professor Hudson said, not bothering with etiquette. "We'll take care of him."

Henry and Wyatt hesitated, but Professor Fowler was already pushing them toward the door. "You've done everything you can. Leave it to us. We'll take good care of him."

Louper practice was supposed to be Luke's favorite—he was better at it than the rest, and he had trained hard over the summer. Get stronger in the real world, get stronger in the virtual world of Louper.

But he was distracted after what had happened to Peter. He felt like shit for not listening to his shifter instincts. He had wanted to look for Peter, but instead, he had let his friends talk him into a meal at the mall.

The outing was fun, especially being with Izzie, but Peter had been hurt. Badly.

And Luke hadn't been there to help him.

"Ready?" Professor Regency asked. He trained them on a regular basis, and Luke liked the guy.

"Ready!" his teammates shouted. The boys were amped and ready to go, all nine of them.

Luke didn't feel ready, but he had to get his head in the game. They had tournaments to win, and he had worked hard to take the first World Cup. Thinking about Peter wasn't going to change anything, and his competitive side would have a fit if he lost at Louper. After all, his muscles twitched waiting to do what he had been training to do.

"Let's do this!" he said through gritted teeth. "For Peter."

The players stood together on the team, the boys looking down the line at each other. Henry, Wyatt, David, Ethan, and Luke were on the team, and they were all fit and ready, along with the others. Professor Regency came striding over to them.

"You boys are doing well. You did great last semester. This semester I want to see you give your all." He waved the clipboard in his hand, getting himself revved up.

The boys all nodded. "I want to give even more this year. The first World Cup is on the line," said Luke. "I know I have more to give."

"I know things are hard sometimes," Professor Regency said, "and we'll keep Peter in mind, but I want you to push it out of your mind for now."

Henry, the team captain, clapped his hands together three times. "All for Cardinals!"

"All for Cardinals!" they shouted in unison.

"All for Peter!"

"All for Peter!" came the loud cheer.

"Let's show 'em how it's done!" Professor Regency saluted them before he stepped away.

The spell was cast, and the field disappeared. They didn't see the playing fields of the school anymore. They weren't even in Virginia. Instead, they stood in a humid swamp in the Louisiana bayou. Luke's instincts trembled. There were stories that the fiercest wolves were created from humans by the dark families of the bayou. He had always been told that the place was filled with its own twisted brand of magic. Louisiana had a whole different breed of witches and wizards, but it was hard to know how many of the stories were true.

"Can't all be true," he muttered, moving through the murky green and black waters that came up to mid-thigh.

A Louisiana heron swooped low overhead, spreading its wings. Its spindly, long legs dangling underneath as it landed farther down the swamp.

"Damn, they go to a lot of trouble to make this game real. Stay ready!" Wyatt waved everyone forward, watching for Henry's next command.

The bayou was filled with ancient magic, and even though it was all just a spell, it felt real, right down to the dank smell.

The team moved through the bayou, searching for the first clue. Luke had been training all summer, running with the pack, and he was strong and lean.

"You're used to these woods, aren't you?" Henry, another senior, grinned at him. A fellow shifter. "We don't have to think about where to put our feet, or which way to turn to avoid the trunks and the underbrush. We can move through the trees faster than our slow elf cousins and wizards slogging it out."

"All right, I get it. You hairy beasts are better than us," said Michael, a Light Elf and another senior on the team.

"Just sayin'," said Henry, stepping up onto dry ground at last, a green film clinging to his skin. The others followed him, keeping their heads turning in all directions. The last players out of the swamp making sure nothing was coming up on them from behind.

"Oooof." Luke tripped over a tree root, rolling head first over the ground. Peter's face flashed before him, and he came to a stop, lying on the ground and breathing hard. He looked up at the blue sky he could see through the canopy of leaves above.

"That was an easy one, dude. Got to get your head into the game. Being that fit, pretty boy, is no good if you can't keep your focus." Wyatt shook his head and ducked low for a branch, still moving.

Focus, dammit! Luke shook his head.

Something big crashed through the trees close to him, and a wild boar showed its face. He jumped to his feet. He was an idiot to lie on the ground for so long in the wild. He heard branches snap. Luke spun around, but it was too late. The boar was going to take him out of the game, and there was nothing he could do about it.

David tackled the boar from the side, leading with his shoulder to knock the boar sideways long enough for him to pour light into it until it blew up, evaporating into the game. The microburst briefly blinded them both. Luke saw stars for a moment and blinked rapidly to clear his vision.

"Thanks," Luke said, rubbing his eyes with two fingers.

David flipped his long, dark bangs to the side. "Don't sweat it."

Luke shook his head. "Should have seen it coming."

"Yeah, you should have…"

He looked up, expecting a reprimand. "No one lost yet, keep it moving, Junior. What? You thought I would bust your balls for it? One of your friends was laid out. I get it."

"Can we have this little lady chat later back at the dorm?" Wyatt rolled his eyes and moved ahead of them, looking for another boar trap.

"Peter will be okay," said Henry. "Singleness of purpose. Be here now."

Luke nodded and let out the breath he was holding. "Get the prize."

"That's right! One intention," David said, clapping Luke on the back. "This is the first worldwide tournament, and we're going to win it."

Luke nodded, and they set off through the cypress and tupelo trees together, meeting up with the others. Luke pushed all other thoughts away and focused on what he did best—tracking.

They found their way through the woods, swatting off mosquitoes and outrunning a boar who finally faded into light particles. Ahead of them was another stretch of bog alive with the sound of bull frogs and the rustle of branches overhead, even as a large black spider crawled across Luke's arm.

"Son of a…!" He knew better than to try and kill it, releasing a deadly gas that would put him out of the game. He bit his lower lip and held his breath, gently scooping the large spider into his hand and setting it on the ground. It immediately dissolved into dust.

"Well played," said David, nodding. "The student becomes the master at Louper."

"Let's keep going, guys. We still have some very soggy road ahead," said Henry.

Well into their second hour they found their way to an abandoned cabin that was being held up by old vines. Luke was feeling the strain in his muscles. Wyatt ventured inside first. His foot broke through the floor, badly scraping the side of his leg. He looked up, shocked, knowing what was already coming as he faded from the scene. He was out of the game, and they were one man down.

"It happens," said Michael, symbols lighting up his arms. He looked down and read the patterns. "We are getting close gentlemen. Stay alert."

A bobcat stepped gingerly into the waters three yards in front of them, a low grumble followed by a scream erupting out of its mouth. The players all instinctively stepped back, except for Luke. He saw what was on its back. "Of course, it's attached to an oversized cat with fangs. Guys, look. It's the prize."

There on the back of the yellow and black spotted fur was the golden disc. "Holy crap! There for the taking!" Luke let out a whoop and a laugh. "Okay, captain, go get it."

"Not a problem," said Henry. "Here kitty, kitty."

The bobcat snarled, making David recoil.

"Yeah, great plan."

"You have a better one?"

"I do," said Luke. "What do all cats hate?"

Henry's face lit up. "Dogs of any kind."

Henry and Luke quickly shifted into oversized wolves as the hair stood up on the bobcat's neck, and he took off at a fast run through the bayou, leading them on a chase. The two wolves easily kept up, gaining on the bobcat till they had it cornered in a thick stand of trees. Luke bared his teeth and growled at the animal as it tried to slash at him with its claws.

Henry circled from the other side as the other team players caught up. He leapt through the air, landing feet first, just as the bobcat faded in the mist, leaving behind the gold disc. Luke and Henry shifted back into human form as Michael leaned down and picked up the prize.

"This is how you do it, gentlemen. Team effort. Go Cardinals!"

"Go Cardinals!" they cheered in return.

The scenery disappeared, the spell faded, and they were back on the field again. The fans in the stands cheered, and the team high-fived and hugged each other, whooping and cheering.

Luke forced a smile, but he suddenly wasn't in the mood. He was tired—more tired than usual, and still worried. He broke off from the team and crossed the field to sit down on the bleachers. He pushed his hands into his hair and scrubbed his hands down his sweaty face. The smell and slime of the bayou were gone, but the sweat was real. He took a deep breath and let it out with a great sigh.

Izzie came to him, and he smiled. He was glad she had come to watch practice. He wasn't in the best space, and she was the one person he wanted to share everything with.

She sat next to him, taking his hand and intertwining her fingers with his. He could tell something was on her mind, but she didn't say anything. She knew he struggled with what had happened, and she would be there for him, for now. He wanted to ask her what was wrong, but he knew she wouldn't tell him until she knew he was all right.

"I'm glad you're here." It was all he needed to say.

"I want to be here for you. Come on, let's go see Peter." She wanted to tell him that the attack on Peter had affected them all, but that could come later.

She could talk to him about her troubles later, too.

CHAPTER FOUR

Alison, Izzie, and Jennifer were on their way to breakfast in the dining room. Jennifer was still thick with sleep, her red hair a wild mess as Izzie yawned. Getting into an early routine after the break was always a challenge, especially when the girls stayed up talking until the early hours of the morning.

Since Peter had gotten hurt, they had spent the night talking about it. The conversation had gone from the attack and the conversation Peter had been on about, to talking about smaller, inconsequential things, but bonding was the best when they were sheltered by the night.

When they passed by the boys' dorm, the doors flung open, and the boys spilled out screaming. The air filled with their panic, lines of icy blue and gray swirling around them in Alison's peripheral vision. Through her glasses, she saw the terrified faces of the boys as they scattered.

The girls stopped dead and sank into a battle stance. Their magic at the ready and prepared to fight. After what had happened to Peter, everyone was on their guard, even though it had happened in town, in a place where he had not been allowed to be in the late hours of the night. They were safe within the gates at the school, tucked away from harm. But still, everyone was shaken up, and doubt lingered in their minds if they were truly safe.

They knew full well what he had been trying to do, even though everyone had thought he'd dropped the subject.

The boys evacuated the dorm and silence filled the air. Izzie let the magic go out ahead of her, looking for whatever dark forces were hiding in the corners for them.

A furry grey head appeared around the corner of the door.

"What?"

A small squirrel ran out, making the girls jump to the side. It squeaked angrily at the top of the stairs before running back into the dorm, and the girls held on to each other, laughing.

"The squirrel chased the boys out again!"

"Maybe it's a changeling. Can a wood elf change that much?"

"I think it's a regular American squirrel chasing off wizards and elves who can throw fireballs if they weren't so busy running away."

"You think they'll ever figure out how to kick out their cranky roommate?"

Alison clutched her chest. Her body felt like it had turned to jelly in the aftermath, adrenaline still pumping through her body.

"These valiant warriors will be our heroes one day."
Izzie snorted.

"As long as our enemies aren't squirrels," Jennifer
quipped. The girls headed toward the dining hall.

"Nice to see you again, Ethan." Jennifer saluted him as
he blushed, ducking his chin and running up the steps in
his pajamas decorated with trolls.

Izzie's mind was filled with what had happened to
Peter. It was the buzz around campus. The girl longed for a
sense of safety. *Family*. Hard to come by when you're an
orphan.

Her thoughts were interrupted by a wave of magic
abruptly rising up her spine. It was so strong that she
stumbled and had to catch herself, putting a hand out to
the nearest wall. It came from the ground, into the soles of
her feet and spread throughout her body. Her eyes glowed,
and the symbols on her arms lit up, flipping over slowly,
searching for information. *Dammit, I am getting sick of being
weird. This shit happens at the worst times. I wish it would
just stop.*

She tugged her sleeves down so the others wouldn't
notice. Just as suddenly, with the new thought, the energy
subsided, and her eyes stopped glowing. The magic was
listening to her inner thoughts.

Alison glanced at Izzie. She knew her friend was trying to
hide it, but Alison could see magic, and no amount of
clothing was going to hide the surge when it pumped
through Izzie's system.

"Are you okay?" she asked.

"Just clumsy." Izzie righted herself and gave a crooked smile.

Alison didn't buy the story. Since the start of the semester, Izzie had been distant like she was listening to an internal voice no one else could hear. No more bursts of chattiness.

"Did I ever tell you about when I found out I was a Drow? It was just before I came to school. No clue before that, can you believe it?" The words hung in the air as they walked to the dining hall.

Izzie pursed her lips, looking away. "The flashes of memory are getting even stronger." She pressed the palms of her hands against the sides of her head. "It's making it hard to know what's real. I mean, I'm not crazy, but what's a crazy magical look like?" The words were coming out in a rush. Alison was grateful that Izzie was finally talking at all and stayed silent.

"It all looks like a movie reel. I can't shake the feeling that there's something missing. It's like I have a puzzle but half the pieces are missing, and the other pieces are all blue sky."

Alison suppressed a laugh. Izzie had a way with words. "How can I help?"

"You're doing it. Thanks for letting me talk and not trying to fix it. That just makes it worse. Besides, some part of me wants the visions. I want to know."

A thought occurred to Alison. "Do you think the magic is trying to help you? Like maybe it feels your truest intention?"

"Yeah, but like a runaway train for magicals with no Starbucks nearby."

———

Jennifer caught up with them, already talking. "Are you going to the Louper game? Let's all sit together. Izzie started to answer as images appeared in her brain, pushing out the sunny day around her. She nodded, "Uh huh," hoping it fit in the conversation and slowed down. It was the back of a woman again, with long dark hair and a tall man. They felt so familiar and so comforting. The toe of her shoe hit against the edge of a tile in the hallway, jarring her back to reality. Jennifer was still talking.

Grace was right behind them and suddenly interrupted, surprising everyone. "I was thinking of doing a study of magical root plants for Professor Fowler this semester. Maybe go into holistic medicine for magicals." She flipped her long, brown hair behind her shoulder, waiting for a response.

Izzie caught on, shaking herself out of it. "Good idea... great idea."

Alison slid her arm around Grace's. "Let's all sit together today. Where's Emma and Aya?"

They neared the dining hall as a student came toward them, batting away at bumblebees.

"Weird time of the year for bees," the student said. "And in the building, too. We can't even keep bees outside."

The images faded again

Alison and Grace, Jennifer and Izzie crossed the wide

tiled floor in the entrance to the dining hall, as Luke joined them.

"Hey, beautiful." Luke took Izzie's hand as she blushed, her skin warming. She liked being with Luke. He was kind and looked her in the eyes when she talked. *If boys ever figure out that just paying attention is the secret to getting girls to like them...*

After growing up in an orphanage—or whatever reality was becoming—Izzie rarely felt like she completely belonged. That wasn't how she felt when she was with Luke or walking at night with Alison.

They sat down at their favorite table, and their plates and bowls of breakfast appeared. Luke pulled Izzie closer, looking her straight in the eye. *Yeah, that works for me.*

His expression was serious, and his voice was low when he spoke. "What's going on?" he asked.

Izzie frowned, the warmth she was feeling draining away. Her stomach tightened. *Okay, not all the time.*

"Nothing," she said, biting her bottom lip. She dug her spoon into the warm bowl of oatmeal, pushing the raisins to the bottom.

Luke shook his head. "It's not nothing. I can see something is up. You can trust me. Talk to me. Let me return the favor. You stood by me last year, and I'll never forget it."

"That was easy to do. The shifters were being persecuted. There's nothing wrong with you; you're just different. Besides, like I said, there's nothing to tell." Izzie shifted uncomfortably in her seat, glancing up at him. *Don't be the strange girl at school.* She looked down at her arm, grateful the magic wasn't chiming in.

Luke sighed and looked around at the other students sitting in groups, talking and laughing. It was clear to him that Izzie had been in trouble for a while now, and he wanted to be there for her. He hated seeing her stand back when she was supposed to be filled with light. She was a beautiful person, and even more beautiful when she was filled with the bubbling wonder she usually radiated. Seeing her so down hurt him because she was hurting.

"Come on, Iz."

Izzie smiled, staring intently at the rest of the oatmeal in her bowl. He grinned, taking a different tack. "Tell me what's wrong. You were here for me when my pack was poisoned. You're here for me with this trouble with Peter. I want to be there for you, too. That's what we do. We're a team. Like Bert and Ernie."

Izzie let out a snort, quickly covering her mouth. "Thank you?" She took a deep breath and looked around.

"Okay, but not here," she said, standing. She took his hand and pulled him behind her to the long hallway that led to the grand staircase and the dorm rooms on the second floor. Just underneath the twist in the oak stairs was an alcove where they could be alone.

The chatter in the dining room faded into the background, and Izzie looked around to be sure they were alone before she started talking. She didn't want anyone to hear what was going on with her. Gossip traveled through the school like a guided fireball.

"I have to ask you this first. Promise me you won't tell

anyone else. Until I'm sure, I don't want to have to explain any of this. You and Alison are the only two who know."

Luke crossed his heart and smiled. "Promise."

"The dreams are getting worse," she finally admitted. "Worse, I don't think they're dreams. I think they're memories."

"Of what?"

Izzie shook her head. "I don't know. People I knew, and I know they cared about me. But I don't know who they are. It's only broken bits and pieces and always fades too fast. But I have this vague feeling like I should know who they are." She hesitated before she added the rest of it. "And my magic is getting away from me." She looked down at her hands. "I don't know what to do." *Please don't look at me differently.*

She slowly looked up at his amber eyes and was relieved to see the same warm concern.

Luke put his hands on her shoulders. "It's going to be okay. We'll figure it out, together. I might even let Alison help."

Izzie nodded as Luke pulled her into a hug, and she wrapped her arms around him. Warmth filled her body, and she felt the powerful shifter heart beating in his chest. "You are always on my side, aren't you?"

"'Bout time you caught on, Izzie. I was beginning to wonder if all that magic was slowing your step."

She pushed against his chest, laughing, feeling a moment of relief.

"Let's go back. I want some more of that oatmeal." Luke took her hand, leading her back down the hall.

At the table, Ethan was busy stuffing a large forkful of

eggs into his mouth with one hand and finishing an essay on his computer pad with the other. Emma was braiding the hair along her face, talking about the upcoming spring dance. "I brought a dress with me, but now I want to look for something else. Something to go with the cherry blossom theme."

Luke leaned into Izzie as he sat down. "No one even noticed we were missing."

"Do you think trouble will interfere with the dance?" Jennifer asked. Everyone had been thinking the same thing, but she had been brave enough to mention it.

"Not here at the school." Kathleen shook her head, determined. "Nothing can happen to us here. It will be fine."

"What do you mean? Plenty has already happened, every year we've been here. This is just getting ratcheted up to a new level of danger." said Ethan.

Some of the others nodded. They all knew what Peter had found. "I mean, okay, I'll say it. Do you think we could be in danger?"

"Nooooo," said Alison, drawing out the word. "Okay, maybe not. Probably not."

"Make up your mind, girl." Ethan stabbed another piece of egg and turned back to typing.

"The headmistress has taken even more precautions. I've heard that freshmen don't sneak out as easily as they once did. Too many glamours and teachers walking the grounds."

"Sucks to be them," said Kathleen.

"Janine," Aya said, waving to a girl from the Entrepreneurs Club who stopped by. Janine's dark hair was pulled back in a neat ponytail, and her uniform was pressed. In her hand, she held a small robot shaped like a fish with arms and legs, chewing on a piece of plastic. Janine was feeding it a steady diet of square bits of plastic.

"What's that?"

"Next big thing," she said, confidently. "Eats plastic non-stop, all day long, every day."

"Where does it all go?" Ethan half stood, straining to see behind it.

Janine picked up the mechanical creature with her other hand and held out her palm. "Poops out pellets that can be made into more plastic, more easily. This is a miniature prototype. Imagine if we got a big one of these?"

"What's with the man-fish design?"

"Nod to Darwin and evolution." She let out a giggle. "How is Peter doing? They won't let anyone visit anymore."

"I tried to go yesterday, and there was a line," said Alison. "The infirmary stopped visitation because it was waking up other patients, but I didn't see anyone else."

"Maybe it was keeping them awake," chortled Ethan. "Big man on campus, who knew nerds rule."

"I knew." Emma raised her hand.

"Me too," said Aya.

Luke rolled his eyes. "He's doing okay." He still felt terrible about what had happened. "He's getting better, slowly."

"Your man-atee is out of plastic," quipped Ethan.

"Hardy har, Ethan. Better focus on your paper. It's half our grade this semester."

Ethan blanched and looked back down at what he was typing.

Janine opened her hand and poured the small round recycled plastic balls into a leather pouch. "Catch you all in class," she said, just as the bell rang for first period.

Ethan snatched one last piece of toast just before the plates and bowls disappeared from the table.

He was trying to get in one more paragraph even as he stood up, taking a bite of toast. There was jelly in the corners of his mouth.

"Done! That was close," he said, gathering up his computer and chasing after his friends.

"Wait up!"

"You know, it doesn't have to be fire drills all the time," said Alison.

"Then where's the reality game show gonna come in?"

"We already have that here, every day. Professors test us by throwing spells at us."

"Yeah, okay, okay," Ethan said, hugging his computer to his chest. "You have a point."

Izzie and Alison left the dining room and turned right to go back to the dorms and pick up their school bags and homework. Alison hoisted her bag onto her shoulder and pulled out her class schedule.

"What do we have first?" Izzie asked.

"History. Something predictable cuz it's already happened. I could stand a little of that right now," Alison said, and they walked out of the room, on their way to class together.

CHAPTER FIVE

"Settle down," Professor Hudson called, and the chatter in her classroom died down. Hudson waited until everyone was quiet, and in their seats, before she sat down on the edge of her table. She looked around at the students. They were growing so fast and getting stronger. Their eyes filled with wonder and excitement about what the future would hold, even in the midst of darkness.

What she had to teach them could make them stronger. *Stronger they are, the more stable their magic. The more prepared they are for reality.*

"Today, I'm assigning internships," she said, folding her hands in her lap.

A ripple of excitement traveled through the class, and she smiled.

"That's right, it's time to head out into the world, just a little," Hudson said with a grin. This was always her favorite assignment to hand out. The students were assigned local magicals to shadow in the hopes they would learn how to use their magic at the right times in different kinds of businesses.

"You will spend two hours every day in the kemana, watching different locals use their powers in everyday settings."

"Like we're normal, or something," muttered Ethan.

"Exactly, because you are." The professor pointed at him. "You can get the first one. You'll be following Mr. Masada who owns a chain of inclusive athletic clubs. He even lets in the occasional willen or troll."

"Sweet!"

"Once you pass this part of the course, we'll move on to companies in Charlottesville. Some are run by humans who are unaware of the special gifts you bring to the table. The goal is to learn to use your powers fully so that you can become selective when you need to."

"Take me next," said Kathleen, waving her hand.

"You are going to help Madame Bella, the local clothing designer. That should be interesting."

Kathleen, delighted and surprised, opened her mouth to say something, but for once she was at a loss for words. The professor took that as a good omen.

"One day, you are all going to leave the school and are going to have to integrate with society. You're going to have to live next door to normies who didn't believe in magic or still don't accept it and may even be suspicious of it.

"No shifting, Luke," yelled Jason Parker, smiling, ignoring the glare from Luke.

"You be you, dude. This is a safe place to be different."

"Learn how to conform without losing what makes you

special. Okay, let's continue." Hudson picked up the stack of papers she'd prepared. On it, there were names and phone numbers of the magicals that were always willing to join the program and help out the kids on their journey to adulthood.

"Alison," Hudson called and held out the documents for pickup. "You'll enjoy this one."

Alison smiled and stood up, walking to the front of the classroom. Hudson liked Alison. The Drow girl had come along nicely since she'd started. She was more confident in who she was, less haunted by her past. She used to be a little wisp of a girl, worried about her place in the world, but had blossomed over the past three years.

"Luke, come on up." Luke's ability to change into an oversized wolf might always be seen as too different, but he was determined to leave his mark without using his claws. He was strong, mixed with kindness, and that was the best combination of all.

"Izzie," Hudson said, and Izzie stood, hesitant. "Come on, child. There's a lot of you, and I need to get all of these passed out before the next bell.

On her way to the front of the class, Izzie shuddered and momentarily lost control of her limbs. She stumbled, and the class chuckled.

"Enough," Hudson said in a stern voice.

The girl stood in front of her and reached for the document, even as her arms lit up with symbols. She jerked her sleeves down, but it wasn't soon enough.

Hudson saw the symbols and could read them. She knew what they were saying. A shock traveled through her as she absorbed the information and figured out what it must all mean.

"Ma'am?" Izzie asked, clutching the paper that the professor was still holding tightly. She cleared her throat, nodding and let go.

Izzie turned and walked back to her seat.

Mara said it was dire, but... Dammit, old friend why did you wait so long? Danger is close, and we don't have much time to prepare.

After Izzie sat down, Hudson swallowed her surprise and continued to hand out the internships. She focused on their enthusiasm, pushing away the new knowledge.

The students were wild with excitement, talking to each other in clipped voices, reaching out and reading each other's papers. But the moment wasn't as wonderful as it should have been.

Professor Hudson knew it was all in jeopardy. But what to do about it...

CHAPTER SIX

The bell rang, and everyone was still talking about their assignment as they filled the hallway, moving past each other quickly before the second bell sounded. Alison and Izzie found their usual seats in the second row of Dark Magic class with Professor Xander Powell.

Professor Powell was good at what he did, and he knew it.

He didn't smile very often, preferring to scowl behind his horn-rimmed glasses. The professor was rumored to have a dark past, which only added to the fables the upper-classmen told the freshman every year. This year there was a story circulating that he used to fight dragons.

But he had a soft spot for every student that walked into his class. He might not be warm and fuzzy, which only made him roll his eyes, but woe to the creature that would bring harm to any of his students.

"When dark magic comes at you, you will need to

counter it quickly, always, and make good out of a bad situation. Literally. You must learn to protect yourselves."

"Seriously," muttered Ethan.

The professor settled his glare on Ethan, pursing his lips but not saying anything. He looked over the class. They were all paying attention.

Since Peter had been attacked in the alley, the class had all developed a sudden interest in dark magic.

"Don't assume that bad things come only from dark magic. We all possess the ability to make a wrong turn. Once you assume, you close your mind to other options. Peter's attackers may have been ordinary humans."

There were gasps and a general shaking of heads. *Maybe they're right, this one time.*

"Okay, well, good. If you're convinced there's a threat, arm yourself with knowledge and practice."

He'd felt the shift in the atmosphere too, but it had been too subtle to identify its origins. Still, times were changing. *Something is coming, and they need to be ready.*

"It's my job to prepare you for the worst, so you don't freeze and get turned into toads."

"Can that actually happen?"

"No, he's just making a point."

"My Uncle Earle said he heard of a fellow at his company that was a toad for a little while."

"There are shifters, so why not…"

The professor clapped his hands together loudly. "We have gotten woefully off track. Pay attention. If things don't go bad, it's a bonus." It was one of his favorite sayings.

"The dark magic isn't going to become your friend

when you use the spell," Powell said. "But it can become neutral. And we can handle neutral."

"Unless it's your crush, and she wants something neutral," Ethan called, grinning broadly. "Boom."

Everyone snickered, even as the professor whispered a spell, spinning Ethan in his chair.

"Dark magic is never a game. Some know it from experience. May that never be you." He pinned Ethan with a cold stare, and Ethan swallowed hard, sinking down in his chair a little with his hand pressed against his belly.

"Right, let's get started." The professor held up his wand and said a spell, swirling a ribbon of magic moving through the air. It hung in a mist around the students, ready to neutralize the dark magic. "We can begin. I want you to learn the spell and say the words—learn exactly how to say it, how to use it, how to conjure it even in a pinch. Then you will react without thinking if you ever come up against it, and you may have a chance of living to see the next day."

He turned his back and smiled, knowing they were all looking nervously at each other with eyes wide. Years of teaching taught him that.

The spell was simple but sufficient to show the students the beginning of what they needed to know. It was dark enough that they had to counter it, and, one by one, Powell called the kids up to try it out for themselves.

Some of them understood the concept right away and did the spell correctly. They neutralized the dark magic, and Professor Powell gave them a nod, eliciting a relieved smile. But some of them didn't know what they were doing at all.

Kathleen slipped up with her magic. Her wand slipped, and a whirlwind escaped, threatening to turn into a tornado, whipping papers, books, and stationery up into a frenzy. The students backed up instinctively even as the mist of protection dampened the indoor storm.

Aya raised her wand, not even thinking, letting out a spark of magic, neutralizing part of the defenses. A column of books slid past the mist and whirled around the students who ducked under the tables. Powell held up his wand, immediately waving it to bring things under control, surprised when it was harder than he expected.

Kathleen was frozen, staring at the results of her spell, not trying to help reel it in.

"Interesting lesson," the professor snarked when he got it under control.

When it was Aya's turn, she tried the spell but lifted herself and a few other students off the ground, instead. "No, not..." She lowered her wand too quickly, dropping them to the hard ground.

Jennifer was at the ceiling; her head bent forward when she started to give in to gravity, rapidly. "Oh," she said, still surprised.

Powell frowned, and was unable to use his wand fast enough. He managed to break her fall, only one of her legs hitting the ground.

She was only mildly bruised. Powell was sprawled on the ground with Jennifer next to him. His back hurt, and he'd bruised his knee. The students applauded. "Yes, well, okay..." He took a nervous bow, almost breaking into a smile.

Aya felt terrible about losing control and went to Jennifer, hugging her.

"I'm so sorry. Are you okay?"

"Hey, next time you want to book a flight, give me a heads-up." Jennifer rubbed her leg, still managing a smile. "For a second there, I was a faerie minus the wings."

"Or don't drop her in midflight," Kathleen chipped in.

Aya looked down at her feet.

"If you've done well, you can afford to comment," Powell snapped.

Kathleen snapped her mouth shut and drew her shoulders up closer to her ears.

When it was Alison's turn, it was easy for her to manage the spell. Powell gave her the satisfactory nod of his head, narrowing his eyes to watch her.

Drow magic.

He was curious about Alison's magic, and how much more she could handle. "You will have an interesting life, Alison Brownstone." He rubbed his trim gray beard with his hand. "Let's see what else you can do" He threw one of his favorite spells on her. It wasn't dark magic, but it was dangerous enough.

The wood under her feet grew unsteady, shaking and turning to liquid, reforming, absorbing and fusing with whatever it was touching.

Alison was quick to act before the floor could congeal around her shoes. She relaxed, focused her energy and pulled out a surprise. Instead of countering the spell, she redirected it, right at Xander Powell.

He was surprised when the spell came back to him. He

easily diffused the spell, but he was surprised at Alison's ease and control.

"Well done," he said, shaking a bit of paper permanently fused to his wingtip. He tapped his shoe with his wand, releasing the paper. Magic changed the definition of permanent.

"You interpreted the situation well, retaliating rather than merely protecting yourself. Bravo. You could be spectacular in a fight, later. You want to be a bounty hunter, right? Interesting."

"Wouldn't it be better if she didn't end up in a fight at all?" Izzie looked at him, defiant. Her inner fight was wearing her out.

"That is a very good question. The answer is, we don't always get to choose. Don't run from life's challenges and prepare while you can. Okay, it's your turn. Step up, come on, no dawdling." He waved his hand, arching an eyebrow.

Izzie swallowed hard.

"It's *your* magic," Powell said. "Embrace it. Don't fear it."

Izzie nodded. He sent magic her way, forming into vaporous, transparent hands pushing her back, shoving over and over again. She furrowed her brow in concentration, her eyes glowing as she set an intention, and the hands disappeared one finger at a time with a pop.

"Well done," he said, nodding.

Izzie relaxed, dropping her shoulders, just as another wave of magic traveled through her, and shot out toward the professor. It made it through the defenses and hit him with a searing hot blast to the chest, throwing him backward against the wall, his head whipping against the concrete.

"Oh, no." Izzie reached out to try and help him. "I'm so sorry."

A murmur traveled through the group. The professor jumped up, as a flash of anger came across his face and his wand raised with the beginning of a spell leaving his lips.

Alison watched in horror, ready to defend her friend if she had to, but he caught himself just in time and cleared his throat, shaking it off.

"It's okay, Izzie," Powell said, forcing himself to be calm, clenching his hand around his wand. "Perhaps you should sit this one out."

Izzie frowned, her shock replaced by anger. *Curious.* The students were usually happy to get a free period.

"Yeah, go cool it down, hothead," someone shouted from the back of the class. Professor Powell snapped his head up, but no one was confessing. Izzie spun around. Her anger danced in the air around them. She knew who it was, and without thinking, she shot a pea-sized fireball toward her offender.

As it traveled through the air, her anger fed it until it grew into a raging ball of fire.

"No!" Izzie cried out, and she reached through the air for the fireball. Too late for simple methods. She quickly set an intention, reaching down deep, and felt her energy build in her stomach. "Help me." She was crying out to the energy, straining toward the fireball, holding her breath as it slowed. Her classmates were all frozen; eyes opened wide.

The fireball paused for a moment, then shot back as if Izzie had yanked on it, hitting her square in the chest. She fell back, and her bracelet from the headmistress slipped off her wrist, falling to the ground.

She moved to pick it up, trembling. She watched it, distracted as the first convulsion hit her. Her body began to spasm, the light shooting up from her feet. The magic was filling every bit of her. She fell to the ground, her eyes glowing a bright white as her rigid body shook. A pulse of energy rolled out from her in waves with a deafening noise. Everyone covered their ears as Alison tried to reach her friend. Plaster from the ceiling rained down on her head, the energy pushing her to the floor.

Izzie lay in the center of it, still convulsing. The symbols spun across her arms, too fast for Professor Powell to read. A look of shock was on his face as he strained against the magical pulse, his arm outstretched to Izzie.

Aya and Kathleen screamed and ducked behind a desk while Emma covered her head and yelped in pain as a shard pierced her hand. Luke growled low, crouched. His muscular build was not enough to overcome the Jasper magic.

Fireballs emerged, hitting the bookshelf, a window, the board, and a stack of tests that were yet to be marked. If it was flammable, it burst into flames.

Some of the students who managed to neutralize the energy Powell had sent their way tried their luck with the fire and put it out as best they could, whispering a spell even as they held onto desks.

Alison ducked around the fireballs, risking being engulfed in flames to get to Izzie and summoning her own Drow energy to crawl across the room.

STRANGE IS HER LIFE

Izzie's eyes were rolling back in her head, and her body was still rigid, the tremors rocking through her as she gritted her teeth. Her body convulsed as a seizure-like attack hit her.

Professor Powell rocked back on his heels, the skin of his face pressed tight from the magic surge. He continued to try one spell after another, watching with a look of amazement at the power surging through the girl. He ducked, too late, and a fireball ran over his shoulder and down his back, burning a line that made him scream in pain. Still, he persisted. He had to help the girl or risk losing her.

As he watched, symbols slowed down on her arms. He froze, reading the symbols.

Oh, no. It can't be possible. It's seeking answers

The bracelet was half-underneath her body. Alison finally reached Izzie in the center of the magic and found a calm spot, putting Izzie's head in her lap and stroking her hair. Drow magic was useless against the strength of the Jasper energy.

Powell stretched, feeling a searing pain across his back and grabbed the bracelet, slipping it onto Izzie's wrist. Finally, her body went limp, and her eyes closed. Ja

"Is she going to be okay?" Alison's voice was shaky, her eyes shining with tears.

"I can't answer that," he muttered. "Class is dismissed," he said tightly and tucked his arms under Izzie, standing with her limp body cradled against him.

"I'll take care of her. Join the others," he said to Alison in a voice as gentle as he could muster. Alison hesitated, wanting to go with her friend, but the professor gave her a cold, hard stare.

Alison felt a chill across her neck and nodded, following her classmates out of the classroom, trusting that her friend was safe.

Professor Powell carried Izzie quickly through the old manor, taking the wide, oak stairs as fast as he dared past the framed paintings of Turner Underwood's relatives. Her body was limp—almost deadweight—scaring him. He kept an eye on her breathing, watching the shallow rise and fall of her chest as the only proof that she was still alive.

It was still class time, and he was glad the other students were still shut away in their rooms and didn't see him carrying Izzie to the infirmary. They would have too many questions, and the news would spread fast. For now, he wanted to keep things quiet till he got answers. He'd deal with the wreckage of the classroom later.

When he arrived at the infirmary, one of the nurses pointed him to a bed, rushing over to him. He carefully put Izzie down on it.

He nodded to Peter, who was still mending in the next bed. When he saw Izzie, he looked worried, sitting up with a grimace.

"What's wrong with her?" he asked.

"She'll be okay." Xander Powell kept repeating the words.

Peter yanked back the curtain separating them and

gasped. "Izzie! What the hell?" His head was still bandaged, and his arm was in a sling, slowly healing.

"She looks worse than I did when they brought me in. Who did this?"

"She did it to herself," barked the professor as Peter's mouth hung open in surprise.

Her skin was ashen, and her eyes were closed. Her hand slipped off the bed and dangled by the side.

The nurse checked her pulse and opened her eye to see if she was still responsive. "She's alive, but barely. What the hell happened? I thought you pulled your punches, Xander!"

She asked one question after the next, but Powell didn't answer them. He kept repeating, "I don't know," over and over.

"How can you not know?" asked Peter, sitting up gingerly, "You know more about dark magic than anyone else in the building. You used to be part of that family!" The words slipped out of Peter's mouth before he could stop them.

Professor Powell uttered a spell between gritted teeth, blowing out the overhead lights, the glass tinkling against the floor. Peter ducked momentarily under the covers, waiting for round two.

"Xander, get hold of yourself!" yelled the nurse. She was white-faced with her wand out and ready. "If you can't control yourself, get out!"

He wiped the sweat off his lip and clenched his fists, letting out a guttural yell, but he didn't move from his post by Izzie.

"Behave. I know a few spells myself." Slowly, the nurse

fussed, complaining under her breath about Professor Powell and his good for nothing nature the entire time, but she found nothing.

"I don't know…" She stopped in mid-sentence as Izzie began to stir. She was coming back to life again. Her eyes fluttered open, and she looked around.

"We may never know what this one's about," the nurse finally said, exasperated.

"You may not know…" The professor leaned over to get a better look at Izzie. The nurse shot Powell a dirty look. "You're not making my job any easier."

"Not trying to." Powell didn't bother explaining any further. He knew he couldn't say anything about what had happened.

"Where am I?" Izzie asked, unsure. "Peter?" Her head pounded, and her body felt weak as if she had done hours of physical exercise. Her body was humming, and muscles were spasming lightly here and there.

"You're bunking with me," Peter said with a grin, leaning out of his bed. The nurse rolled her eyes and gently pushed him back against his pillows. "Down boy."

Izzie stared at him before looking around, finally realizing where she was. "What am I doing in the infirmary? What the hell happened?"

"You blew up a room with your classmates in it."

She glanced at Professor Powell, who stood next to her bed with a scowl on his face.

"I'm sorry. I don't know what I've done, but," she looked at his worried scowl, "it must have been something. Was there a fire?"

"A fire!" The nurse ran to find someone to go check on

the room. Professor Powell watched her go, glad to have the room to himself, despite Peter.

"It was an old room, due for a makeover. I never cared for the seating arrangement, anyway." It all sounded like a bark. Izzie wasn't sure how to take it.

"Stay here, at least for the afternoon. I'll have Alison bring you your homework."

"That's the Professor Powell we all know and quake in front of." Powell whipped around and glared at Peter who pulled the covers back over his head. Izzie managed a crooked smile.

Powell didn't say anything else. Instead, he turned on his heel and marched out of the infirmary.

"Where are you going?" called Peter. "I have more questions. This would make a great piece for the newspaper!"

CHAPTER SEVEN

Xander Powell hurried through the wide halls of the old manor. The chestnut panels on the wall were polished to a sheen, and the old portraits seemed to be watching him as he rushed along. He stepped around the odd glamoured broom sweeping up the dust and shook his head at a squirrel standing on the edge of an old bishop's chair, idly eating an old, stray Doritos.

He came around the corner to the stairs and took them two at a time, climbing toward the fourth floor and the headmistress's office. He had a bone to pick with her, and he was not in a good mood.

He reached the office and was about to storm in when a bloodcurdling scream raised the hair on the back of his neck.

"Graaaaaaaaggggh!"

The scream had come from another part of the building. He hesitated for just a second. "Dammit!" he hissed, his hand hovering over the curved brass handle.

But when the screaming didn't stop, he spun around and ran in the direction of the sound.

Mara burst out of her office, right on Powell's heels. "Xander?"

He glanced back, frowning. "Not now!"

They arrived at one of the small courtyard gardens and the source of the screaming. A dazed sophomore named, Sophie lay on the ground, rocking back and forth, her eyes closed, her dark hair covering her face. She was still screaming, pausing only to take a breath before she carried on.

"Whatever her problem is, it's all in her head. She's physically fine." Xander stood over her, scanning for any sign of a wound, or a spell clutching at the girl. There was nothing.

Sophie appeared to be alone, the sun shining down on her in the small courtyard garden of enchanted roses always in bloom. Aside from the screaming girl, nothing was out of place.

"What's wrong with her?" Mara called over the noise that filled the air and was attracting a steadily growing crowd of students. She kneeled next to Sophie and gently shook her. "Open your eyes, child!"

Sophie was completely oblivious to her surroundings. "Be aware, be present," Mara said the spell in a stern voice. It was one of her most used at the school and powerful, but nothing. Sophie was stuck in a different world, and nothing Mara did could bring her out of it.

"It's a magical attack," Powell yelled. He kneeled beside Mara and pulled out his hickory wand.

"What else is going to go wrong today?"

"Else?" Mara looked up and saw the anger in his eyes. "What else has happened?"

"Apparently legions of things that no one has bothered to tell me. But not now! Focus!" He put his hand on her head and closed his eyes. "Horrible images that seem real. It's a spell, like night tremors, but worse."

He could feel the dark magic inside of her. The spell affecting her mind was creating evil creatures that terrified her, making her believe they were all real. "She believes she's in hell. A particularly nasty little spell. If she's lucky, she will walk away from this kind of terror without mental damage. Fear like this is hard to recover from if the student has a weak mind."

"Two moons," gasped Mara, ashen. "The darkness has gotten inside the school grounds, again."

He put both hands on her head and started whispering, trying to break the spell. It was hard to concentrate while the student screamed and writhed under the touch of his fingers. He was aware of the students around him, and the group was growing. Everyone wanted to see what was going on. He struggled to focus with the dark magic, the students' interference, and the screaming, and he was getting more agitated by the moment.

"Get them out of here!" he shouted. The pressing students were only making it more difficult. Their anxiety and curiosity created a mixture of energy that Powell had to fight through to get to the girl's mind.

Mara clapped her hands and gestured for the students to leave. Professor Hudson rushed in, quickly assessing what was happening, the look of horror growing on her face. "Come on. Everyone out!" She waved at the students, shouting at everyone to move faster

"First Peter, and now this? What is happening?" She looked at Xander as he did his best to break the spell.

"Whoever did this is practiced in the dark side of magic. It's clinging to her everywhere and has taken root in her imagination."

"*You* are practiced in dark magic."

He kept his attention on the swirling darkness inside the girl's mind. "This is on a whole new level. I walked away a long time ago, and apparently, the dark families have been creating new twists to old favorites. It's always harder to fight it than to practice it. I'm doing what I can."

When Mara came closer, he looked up at her with an angry face.

"Get back! You've done enough," he snapped, turning his attention back to the girl.

Mara swallowed hard but did as she was told. "You know, don't you?"

He didn't answer.

Finally, Powell got the spell under control. Mara felt the energy snap as he broke through the spell. A transparent, shimmering wave of magic rippled over their heads, and the girl's screams turned to sobs. She had seen terrible things, and she lay on the ground, limp. Her mind was nearly torn apart by the image, and her soul almost shattered by fear.

"I don't believe she has entirely lost herself. She has managed to hold on to her sanity."

"What happened?" Mara asked as Sophie pushed up on one elbow, trembling all over. Her cheeks were stained with tears, and her pupils were dilated. She looked around as if she wasn't sure where she was.

"Two wizards," she said, hiccupping. Her fingers trembled as she lifted one hand to her face. "They were on us before we knew what was happening."

Mara frowned. "Us?"

The student looked around, anxiety permeating the air around her.

"Where's Lisa?" She craned her neck, fear riddling her features. "Did they take her? Lisa!" She was getting hysterical again.

"Lisa's her roommate. They're always together."

Mara whipped around to see Scarlett, the student body president, standing in the courtyard, her wand at the ready. "The two are never seen one without the other if they can help it. It's a little much, but if one of them isn't here, she's missing."

Sophie was trembling and looking around frantically. She was on the verge of screaming again.

"They took her," Sophie wailed. "They took Lisa and left me with the nightmares."

Xander's stomach tightened. "How is this possible?"

"Scarlett," Mara said quietly. "Inform the library gnomes we've had a breach." Mara glanced back at the students pushing past Eleanor Hudson, looks of concern and fear on their faces. "A student may be missing."

"May be missing?" snarled Xander.

Scarlett nodded and turned to go, stopping to share her opinion loudly. "Maybe if some students acting as junior journalists didn't meddle in business outside the school, this wouldn't have happened."

"She has a point. Peter may have caused them to up their game." Xander was breathing hard, looking down at Sophie. "Enough!" he shouted, shaking Sophie out of her hysteria, if only temporarily.

"That's quite enough," Mara said in a low, stern voice. She was filled with quiet anger, and it reached with dark fingers to Scarlett, who was pressing her lips together. "Students are hurt, and you're mocking them. That's not acceptable in any way. Get out of my sight before I think of a punishment that will last the entire semester. Your last semester."

Scarlett snapped her mouth shut and turned on her heel, hurrying away to do as she was told.

Scarlett moved quickly through the hallways until she reached the library. "What just happened?" she muttered. "Hey, hello..." She passed two girls from her dorm, opening her mouth to spill the best gossip she'd ever had, but something made her hesitate. "Apparently, I do have limits when it threatens the school. Who knew?" she whispered.

She ran into the library, looking in every direction.

"Can I help you?" Leo Decker, the head librarian said in an annoyed tone.

"A message from the headmistress. Security has been breached. A student may be missing."

The poppy on the gnome's bowler growled at her, baring its sharp, pointed teeth.

"I agree, and it's not okay," she said tightly, responding

to the growl. "Apparently, not everyone around here can follow the rules."

The gnome eyed her. Scarlett took a deep breath. "She'll be okay though, right? You can get her back?" She didn't like that danger was creeping closer and closer.

"We'll do what we can," Leo grumbled, tapping his fingers against his forehead. He cleared his throat and said in a voice loud enough to be heard throughout the library. "Gather! A breach! Gather!"

Heads popped out of the aisles in different spots as the gnomes looked to see if it was a false alarm.

"Gather! Gather!" Leo shouted, clapping his hands together.

The library gnomes scurried out of the aisles, grouping together, their arms around each other's shoulders, with their heads in the center. They were in charge of the magic that protected the school.

"Go to the north line, Mel," commanded Leo. "And take two librarians with you. Felix, you take the south line. Everyone else, split into two groups. One to the gates and the other near the buildings. Look for the girl, look for intruders, and test the spells. This may only be the beginning!"

Scarlett stood to the side, unsure what to do now that her job was done.

"I'm headed to the basement," yelled Professor Annabelle Grant, her willow wand waving through the air in front of her. Scarlett recognized the finder spell and watched the ribbon of magic curl out of the top of the professor's wand.

More teachers were also running down the hallways,

shouting at each other, calling out for Lisa Elizabeth May in the hopes that she was somewhere in the hallways, passed out or caught in terrors herself, or hiding from the dark magic that had somehow found its way into the walls of the school.

CHAPTER EIGHT

Alison and her friends gathered in front of the library.

"We can't just stand around and do nothing," said Jennifer.

"Yeah, we have a stake in this too," said Luke. Grace and Claire nodded in unison. Claire sat there, waiting for Scarlett, glancing over her shoulder.

"Let's think this through," said Jason Parker, licking his lip nervously. "I mean, the teachers are handling things, right?" Ethan glared at him, and Jason held up his hands in front of himself. "Okay, okay. How can I help?"

Tanner rolled his eyes and turned his back. "We need to organize and stay in touch with each other."

"I agree," said Alison, squeezing his hand. "I have a hunch I want to try. Tanner, can you ask Dorvu for help? The dragon can cover more ground faster and even fight off any intruders. Come on, Kathleen, you and I are going to search the library." Izzie was still in the infirmary, so she was going to have to call on her other friends as backup.

Jason blanched, his eyes widening. "Is that wise?" he practically squeaked.

Alison's eyes narrowed, and she looked at him, studying his soul. The small stream of darkness swirled inside of him. She stared at him, waiting for more, but he looked down at his shoes and said nothing more.

"I don't have time for this." She grabbed Kathleen's hand, and they strode into the library. Only three gnomes were left protecting the stacks. "We have a chance to find something."

Kathleen easily distracted the gnomes. She dropped a book and put it back in the wrong place, quickly turning a corner, leading them behind her down different stacks of books, and making loud excuses.

"Ack!" The poppies spat and growled at her, hissing.

"Hope this works," whispered Kathleen. "Go, Alison."

Alison ducked, avoiding a gnome searching the next stack over. She worked her way through the books, making her way toward the edge of the restricted area where the darker spells books were kept. A gnome stood firmly in the center of the three aisles with his arms crossed over his chest, looking from right to left.

Kathleen passed right in front of him, pulling a random book off a shelf and walking quickly away.

"Hey!" he yelled, chasing after her.

Alison saw her chance and slipped into the restricted

section's cage, quickly searching the titles. She was sure it was a spell they were looking for rather than an artifact that caused the trouble. A spell could be whispered, and it would work long after the person who cast it disappeared. But the only way to find out was if she could find confirmation in the books. Professor Powell had taught them last year that terror spell books were mostly written well over a century ago by witches from Oriceran, giving her an idea of where the gnomes catalogued them.

She had to move quickly through the stacks, running her fingers over the braille on the shelves, using the glasses as she whispered a spell to help her read them.

She felt a label and went back, ducking at the last moment and pressing herself against the shelf as Kathleen shouted a few aisles over, "Hey, did you see that? I think I saw something!" The gnome hustled off to investigate as Alison let out a deep breath.

"Contour spells, got it! That helps with the perimeter question—how anyone could have gotten inside to take a student and attack Sophie. But what were they looking for and is it over?" Alison pulled the book off the shelf and tucked it under her shirt.

Kathleen went jogging past her, a gnome in tow. She glanced at Alison, who gave her a small wave and quickly pointed at the door. Alison made her way there, and Kathleen slipped past the gnome, meeting up with her.

"There has to be more dark magic locked in the vault," Alison said.

"We'll never get in there. Did you find anything?"

Alison tapped the book under her shirt. They looked over their shoulder at the shouting in the hall outside the library as the teachers frantically ran around looking for Lisa.

Professor Grant had finished her search of the basement and came into the library. Alison and Izzie froze.

"Here you are," she said, sounding relieved. "We were worried Lisa wasn't the only student that disappeared. I've been doing a roll call. You have to take shelter, all of you."

Professor Cooper walked in behind Grant and quietly spoke to her. Grant fell quiet, listening. The girls took the opportunity to walk away unnoticed.

"There may be more wizards still on the grounds," whispered Miles Cooper.

"How could this be?" she said. "I searched the basement but found nothing"

"There's no sign of them leaving. The ground's perimeter spells should have shown evidence of that, but there was nothing. The student couldn't have just vanished. We have to expect the worst."

"And hope for the best." Grant patted her chest, breathing deeply. "This is bad. Did anyone check for signs a portal was used or try a locator spell? Didn't they find anything?"

Cooper shook his head, "Nothing."

She swallowed hard and shook her head. "They could have carried her off," she said. "What about the main gate? The old-fashioned way, they just walked out."

Cooper gave her a level stare, and she knew it was unlikely. "No one saw a thing. Besides, the protection spells surrounding the grounds would have set off the alarms. We would have all heard it."

Outside magicals were only allowed past the magic barriers when they had an appointment. The wards were all very carefully cast, taking hours of complicated spells and ancient words put together in the right sequence.

"Well, we should have been alerted if someone breached the perimeter *anywhere*. And that didn't happen."

"This is bad," she repeated. "Where could someone be hiding right under our noses?" She took a deep breath and tried to stay calm, but panic rose in her throat, and she had to swallow it down. "I have to go," she said, squeezing Cooper's arm. "Use the magical relay system to let me know if you find something. That has to still be secure."

"I'll search the basement again. There has to be something. You know I can do a better job of blending in to the background." He was a wood elf and could melt right into the scenery, the four pupils scanning at the same time. "It'll be okay. I'll report back along the relay."

Miles Cooper watched Professor Grant, hoping she was wrong.

He moved through the building to the stairs, scanning for anything that was out of the ordinary as he headed for the basement's entrance. At a school for magical teenagers, spotting *out of the ordinary* wasn't as easy as it sounded.

Professor Cooper had to pay attention to the atmosphere, to the miniscule shifts in energy that could tell him what he needed to know. *Nothing*. Everything was exactly the same.

"That's what's unusual."

He heard the screech of the dragon and ran outside where he spotted Horace, the groundskeeper. "Good. Horace! We need every hand on deck." Horace waved and went back to what he was doing. He was talking to the dragon, pointing to the forest with his dog by his side patiently waiting. The dragon flapped his wings and pushed off from the ground. The large wings whipped up a cloud of dirt as the body lifted into the air. Dorvu was quickly soaring just under the clouds.

Horace knelt in front of his dog and held up a purse belonging to Lisa, releasing him. The dog barked and ran into the distance, Horace at a run behind him, barely keeping up. The dog was chasing something.

Cooper gave up on the basement and followed Horace and his dog, his skin shifting and changing to match the passing background. He was moving fast, keeping up at a run as Horace, the dog, and the dragon crossed the grounds.

Dorvu landed with a loud flap of his wings and emerged with something in his silver muzzle. Horace took it and studied it.

It was a school sweater with Lisa May's name tag sewn into the collar. The sweater was torn, evidence of a struggle, but there was nothing else.

Professor Cooper caught up and looked over his shoulder, holding his breath.

No blood, thank God.

Horace rubbed the sweater between his fingers, thinking.

Cooper let his skin settle back into its natural resting state—a deep brown color. His pupils moved in different directions looking for any other clues, no matter how small.

"Whoever did this had to have help from the inside. There was no other way. The trail ended with nothing else, no sign, no magical trail."

"It's a puzzle," said Horace.

"A sign of more trouble to come. Someone had better tell the headmistress and the sooner, the better." Cooper left to head back to the main building to help lock down the school even tighter, if that was possible.

CHAPTER NINE

Alison was determined to find out more and use her Drow energy. She wanted to see what she was really capable of doing.

She could see souls, auras, and magic. It allowed her an edge that no one else at the school had, including Kathleen. They had split up. Kathleen took the upper floors ready with a fireball already formed in her hand. Alison headed for the lower floors, using the glasses and occasionally stopping to take them off, so she could focus on the lingering trails of magic.

As she walked down the hallway on the first floor, passing the empty dining hall, she focused on the magic that was always in the floors and the walls, built up over the years that brought the school building to life in a way no one else could see. The colors were as beautiful as ever, jewel tones lighting up the entire building. She stopped, snapped out of her reverie.

A new trail of magic was visible like messy UV footsteps on a dark floor.

Alison started following the trail down the hall, slipping into a classroom as two professors came barreling toward the far front door, running outside. She glanced around and didn't see anyone else.

She went to the door and opened it just enough to see where they were running. *Have they found something?*

Teachers were moving in different directions, some stopping to talk to each other quickly and split off again. *Nothing.*

She was about to let the door close but spotted a faint trail of magic, and she crept out to get a better look. *A student was out here with them. Friend or foe? Another victim?*

It blended in and joined the main trail, both leading back to the building.

Alison went back inside, and focused on the trail, shutting out the rest of the world. The trail was fading faster than she could follow it. Something was erasing the trail—another spell. "Someone is trying to cover up their tracks."

There were so many old spells absorbed in the walls and the floors of the school that it was slowing down the erasing spell, allowing Alison to get closer to an answer. She summoned her Drow magic, assisting the trail to keep it alive just a little longer.

Her head was down, and she was so focused that she ran right into Professor Xander Powell. "What? Who?"

The professor looked startled and stepped back just as Alison realized he was conjuring a spell. She could see the magic swirling around him, and she gasped. "Dark magic."

The words left her before she had a chance to think. "You? But I trusted you."

"It's not what you think." Powell blanched as Alison took a step back, calling on her Drow power to shove him back against the wall, pinning him there.

It was all he could do to speak. "Stop! You don't understand." The words came out slowly and tortured. "Nooooo. Don't!"

She hurried down the old steps to the basement, batting away cobwebs, pushing aside an old, broken desk and weaving her way in the labyrinth of old stone hallways, sensing her way and prepared to fight.

The trail stopped at a wall too thick for her to read any energy. She ran her hands along the cool, smooth stone, pressing as hard as she could, desperate for any kind of clue. "No, no. There has to be something." She pounded against the stone, whispering spells she learned in class to open hidden doors. The wall remained as solid as ever.

She looked back at the dimming trail. *What did Dad tell me?* If you want to become a better bounty hunter, follow the low-hanging fruit first.

Alison ran as fast as she could, tripping over an old broom handle, catching herself just in time, retreating back along the trail as fast as she could back up the stairs. She stopped suddenly when she noticed that Professor Powell had escaped her energy. "Can't worry about that now."

She ran down the hall, keeping an eye out for the professor, and up the stairs toward the boy's dorm. She didn't let herself think about who she might find next. Who else had betrayed the school?

The trail vanished when she reached the floor. She was too late, after wasting time wrestling with Powell and finding her way through the basement. She couldn't tell which room it had led to. There was nothing more than the normal school magic everywhere. The trail had faded completely. She looked around, trying to find the trail again or at least a couple of clues that she could follow.

"Hey, slow down." Jason Parker nearly ran into her. He seemed unsettled, his magic trembling. Alison felt a shiver over her skin. He looked uneasy, but he flashed her a grin. Handsome as ever, Jason had charm on his side, and it let him get away with a lot. But this time, she was suspicious. Alison smiled back at him. She was still wearing her glasses and could see his easy charm, the way he hooked his thumbs in his pockets and grinned.

But something else drew her attention, too. Jason was attractive and charming, but something dark swirled inside of him, and it was bigger than before. Darker than before. This pointed to something, but she had no proof.

"Have you heard about Lisa?" she asked. Maybe his reaction would give her something to work with.

Jason nodded. "It's a terrible thing that happened."

Alison watched his reaction closely. "I was supposed to find Professor Powell, but he ran out of the main hall." Jason's eyes widened for a moment, but he recovered quickly.

His grin was evaporating, but his aura was disturbed.
Wrong answer, asshole.

"I have to get going," Alison said, wanting to get out of there. Her mind was buzzing, trying to wrap itself around the possibilities, and she was struggling to stay civil. "I have to get out of here." The darkness inside of him looked familiar. Professor Xander Powell.

"See you around," Jason said, not wasting any time, running in the other direction.

CHAPTER TEN

"You didn't find anyone?"

Izzie sat on her bed, released from the infirmary with orders to take it easy.

"No, and I kept at it all day. Professor Powell was nowhere to be seen."

"Did you tell Headmistress Berens?"

"I tried, but she kept telling me I was wrong. I didn't know everything and told me to leave things to the adults."

Izzie smiled. "But that's not gonna happen."

"Hardly. This is our school, too. I'm not going to sit around, waiting for the danger to find us. Besides, after what Peter heard last semester…"

"You wonder if one of us is next."

"I wonder if we were the real targets."

"Who knew losing control and passing out would be the slow news for the day." Alison started to say something, but Izzie waved it away. "I'm fine. I'm over it even if someone still wants to talk about it. We need to figure out what's happened to Lisa Mays. Nothing else matters."

"You up for a late-night walk?"

"You know it. Let me get my coat," she said, throwing back the covers. She was already wearing pants, getting a laugh from Alison.

Alison and Izzie snuck out of their dorm. Gnome guards were posted at intervals down the hallway, but the girls managed to get past them unseen, thanks to Alison using her Drow energy.

It was good to get out into the crisp air. Since the start of their stay at the School of Necessary Magic, Alison and Izzie had snuck out for midnight strolls across campus, and with everything going on, Alison wanted to clear her head.

"It feels good to do something that's anywhere near normal," said Alison, looking up at the night sky through her glasses, marveling at the stars.

The moon was almost full, bright and calm in the inky sky. No matter what happened on the Earth below, the moon never changed, and it brought Alison a sense of peace.

"No one thinks it's very safe for us to be wandering around out here at night."

"I don't have a sense of foreboding, and it has been too long. Izzie, I was so worried about you. I'm glad we're out here. Besides, we can take care of ourselves, right? Hit me high!" She held up her hand, and Izzie laughed, smacking her hand.

"You are pretty badass."

"The light is on in the barn. Horace is still up."

"He might actually rat us out this time, or Estelle will."

"Let's chance it. I want to see if he knows anything."

Dorvu landed nearby, snorting blue ice crystals. "Go back inside," he said. His voice had changed into a deep baritone, but he still saw the girls as family.

Alison rubbed her hand along the smooth, silver scales wrapping her arms around his neck for a hug. "We'll be okay. Keep watch above us. We need this."

"Very well," he said, stepping back. "But I'll be watching."

He flapped his wings, blowing back their hair as he took flight with a screech.

"Actually, that makes me feel better," said Izzie, watching the dragon soar, making large circles.

"Wait!" Alison put out her arm, stopping Izzie in her tracks. "Look who it is! Still think he is innocent?"

Professor Powell came around a corner, and Alison and Izzie jumped behind the tall boxwood.

Xander Powell was clearly angry. Alison watched him throw off dark red streaks that were filled with turmoil. There were other colors, too. Regret, a little fear, frustration.

"Dammit, only a few more minutes. If I'd only gotten there sooner," he muttered to himself, shooting off sparks and flames that fizzled out and crashed to the ground, leaving small indents in the grass. He passed right by the girls, too lost in thought to see them.

"We should see where he's going," Izzie whispered.

Alison shook her head when he was far enough away not to hear her. "Too dangerous."

"Is there a chance that he's innocent?"

"At this point, anything is possible. Look, if he is and catches us outside, he'll take us to Mara, and we'll never be able to come out at night again."

"I didn't think about that." Izzie nodded. Alison was right, and she didn't want to give up the bit of freedom they got when they were out at night away from everyone and everything else.

Alison hesitated, clearing her throat.

"What is it? I know that tactic. Spill it, Alison."

"I think Jason is the mole," she blurted in a jumble of words. "I know. I know. It seems crazy, but I found a trail of magic that led to the boy's dorm and I found him lurking nearby."

"That guy has always given me the creeps, and besides, I trust you, I'm in. Let's figure it out. What's first?"

Alison reached out and squeezed her friend's hand. "I'm so glad you're here. I know he's the key, but I don't know how to find out if it was real, without asking him outright. I haven't been able to find anything else. You're trusting my gut."

"A Drow instinct, don't discount that. If we just confront Jason, and he really is behind everything, then he might disappear, and that would be the end of it. We might never find the truth and put Lisa and maybe others at risk."

"Maybe us you mean."

A twig snapped, and Izzie spun around, drawing in her magic, ready to fight. There was still danger around, and the two girls were a lot more on edge than usual.

"Nothing will go wrong, right?"

"Right, keep saying that." Izzie's eyes glowed in the darkness.

Tanner stepped out of the darkness, just as Izzie flung a fireball in defense.

"Tanner!" She scrambled to draw the energy back in, practicing what Professor Powell had taught her while she was in the infirmary. He had said it was likely going to come in handy.

When she couldn't do it, she changed the fireball's direction instead. It burst a young sapling into flames. Alison helped by using her own Drow magic to put it out.

Thank God for friends like Alison.

Izzie was a little tense. It was the first time since she'd stepped out of the infirmary that she'd used her magic, and she was nervous about everything that had happened. A dangerous combination while wandering around in the dark.

She'd told herself she was over it, but maybe she hadn't dealt with it the way she'd thought she had.

"Let me help you," said Alison.

The sounds of the shifter pack howling echoed in the distance.

"What was that?" Tanner asked, ducking again.

The sound was as eerie as it was beautiful. It was wild and free.

"It's Luke," Izzie said. "He snuck out with the pack. They're running as wolves tonight, looking for Lisa." The two girls weren't the only ones who were out when they shouldn't have been.

Everyone had decided to jump in and help in any way they could. None of the students had wanted to sit back and wait for the professors to do something about Lisa's disappearance. They were all being educated in the art of magic, and they could use as many people as were willing to get involved—even if the professors would rather the students stayed safe in their dorms.

"I want to help, too," Tanner said. He turned to Izzie. "I want to help you."

Izzie frowned.

"I think I know what spell was used to take away your memories," he continued, glancing at a confused Alison. "I didn't say anything because I'm not sure it can work."

Izzie looked up when Tanner said it. "How did you know?"

"Alison may have told…"

"Never mind. Spill it, I'm tired of feeling crazy."

"I think it was someone powerful who would have access to older, dark magic. A witch or wizard, one of my own kind."

Alison took Tanner's hand, picking up on the angry vibes that he was throwing off.

"I'm glad you're out here with us."

"Tell me about the spell," Izzie said.

Tanner nodded, taking in a deep breath and relaxing his shoulders. He held onto Alison's hand as he loosened up. "I think someone locked up your real memories somewhere," he explained, and Izzie felt her stomach drop. "They're being held somewhere."

"How can memories be held? They're not a thing."

Tanner shrugged. "It's magic, I guess. I don't know how it works exactly, but it's a lot like the same way an artifact is given magic from different sources."

"The object absorbs the magic," gasped Alison.

"Exactly. I read up on it, and I found out a few things.

They'll look like a shiny ball and probably be kept some-where safe like in a spelled box or a bag. Small enough to hide pretty easily."

The words were crazy, but Izzie somehow knew this was true. She didn't know how she knew, but it was some-thing in her gut that she couldn't shake. "Who would do something like that to me?"

"Answer that, and we would solve the whole mystery," said Alison.

"What do you know that is so valuable someone wanted to steal them away from you?" Tanner peered into the darkness.

"I have so many questions. The problem is that's all I have."

"For some reason, the spell is failing," Tanner said. "I'm not sure why—it looks like it held up at least since you got to school. What, three years ago? Whoever did it, did it well enough that even your Jasper energy couldn't break through at first. But that's all changing now. Your magic is doing its best to help you."

It was so much to take in Izzie's head spun. "You've been a lot of help, Tanner. Thank you, but I'm no further ahead, not really. Aside from knowing that my memories were taken, I still know nothing."

"We know we're looking for a container." Tanner kept turning around, looking in different directions.

"Are you looking for someone?" asked Alison.

"Just trying to stay on guard."

"You think the dark forces are after one of us, don't you?" Alison arched an eyebrow.

"Don't you?"

"How do you know any of this?" Izzie asked.

"Because of this." Tanner swapped hands with Alison and pulled out a folded-up piece of paper out of his back pocket. He handed it to Izzie who unfolded it, gasping. The paper was thick parchment from one of the original magic books, not one of the reprints that filled the library. The symbols on the page were neat, drawn in ink with something like a quill. It wasn't printed. Her eyes scanned the page curiously. She gasped when she saw what it was.

The page had been torn out of a book. One of the edges was shredded.

"How did you get that?" Alison demanded to know. She didn't have to look at the page to know that it was riddled with old magic.

"This is from a book belonging to Professor Powell." Izzie touched the paper, feeling the vibration of dark magic. "That doesn't make sense. Why would he damage one of his own books if he's part of this?"

"You took the book…" Alison stared at Tanner, hoping for a good explanation.

"I only took one of the books. I don't know what the rest is about, and I had a good reason." He held up his free hand, nodding. "Look at it! It's a spell that can help you remember."

Alison shook her head. There was no telling what Professor Powell would do if he found out what Tanner had done. "You've put yourself in danger, too."

"Izzie's my friend, and we all need to stick together."

Izzie was already caught up in what she was reading.

Alison knew that this could be the answer her friend was looking for. Despite her worry that Powell would likely put them in detention for the rest of their school career, she was as curious about what this could mean for Izzie.

Izzie read the words, trying to decipher what it meant. "Ipsum, radium..." The symbols were old and difficult to decipher. She looked up, excited. "We've touched on this kind of magic a few times in spell class. Last year, I think," squinting as she read the words again. "We can do this."

Slowly, she was working it out. The shifters howled in the night. Their cries came from a different direction. They were circling the grounds.

"It's a big spell; stronger than anything we've learned to do before." Doing it would take a lot of energy and could drain Izzie. And after her recent spell, that could be dangerous.

But if she was going to remember, then she wanted to give it a go. She was willing to take the chance. This could mean everything would change. This could mean she would finally know who those two people were who she saw in her waking dreams.

"How do we do it?" Alison asked, sensing Izzie's determination. "Don't worry. Whatever it takes, I'll be right next to you, helping."

"We need a lot of power," Izzie said, still reading. "We'll have to join hands to do it." She looked up at Alison and Tanner. "If you're both willing to help."

Alison and Tanner nodded. "Whatever you need."

"We help each other, no matter what."

"If it's the last good thing we do," said Izzie, surprising herself. The words felt more like a memory.

"Then let's get started. What do we do first?"

"It says to join hands to increase the energy."

Tanner put out his hand, connecting with Izzie, the three of them standing in a small circle. Izzie closed her eyes and started chanting the words of the spell. "Ipsum, radium, allegeran…Shifting, shifting…"

Alison and Tanner only listened to her repeating herself once before they caught on, remembering the words, and joined in, shutting their eyes. The heat grew in their palms, fusing them all together, the magic whipping around in a circle and through each of them. Izzie arched her back, the bracelet barely holding back her own magic.

"This is big," whispered Alison. She opened an eye to peek and saw the color of the power was a bright white light, brighter than anything Izzie had ever given off herself. "We have to be on the right track."

Magic grew inside the circuit, the power building into something bigger than any one of them individually would have been able to handle. Tanner was being pulled up onto his toes.

"It's working," shouted Izzie, the symbols along her arms flipping over, glowing. The power became so strong that it was all Izzie saw, all she breathed. The light flowed around and through them like water, as if they had become light. It was a warm sensation like they were floating. Izzie gave herself over to the sensation, losing herself in the magic, dazzled by the light.

"Wham! Whomp!"

The power blew out, the light blowing out, knocking them back. They tightened their grip as the magic swirled into the air, sparking and blowing up between the three of them.

"Son of a…"

They all cried out in unison and stumbled, but they didn't let go. Izzie wasn't sure if it was because they wouldn't or if they couldn't. Memories flowed between their hands, sliding along the light that connected them, and suddenly, no one's memories belonged to only them anymore.

Childhood birthdays, being rescued by Brownstone, growing up in an orphanage, following behind the dark-haired woman. It was a jumble of memories.

They were sharing each other's conscious. The three of them were connected in a way none of them had ever seen. Alison forced her eyes open and saw the energy of their souls was fused together, swirling in a rolling ribbon of color.

"It's beautiful…" Her voice was lost in the sound of the rushing light.

They were light-headed. The world felt like it was tipping on its axis, and they swayed as one.

"What am I seeing?" Alison asked. "Wetting a bed in the orphanage? Jeering kids?"

Tanner cleared his throat, cheeks burning red, and along with the memories, she could feel the embarrassment.

"Yeah, that's my memory." It was hard to hear him.

It was strange to be connected like this, to share energy as if there was an open flow between the three of them. Tanner looked uncomfortable, but Alison squeezed his hand. He felt the sensation of her acceptance more than she could ever have said to him in words. The connection between them was spectacular.

When Alison looked at Izzie, she knew that Izzie had felt the same memory, seen the same images. The three of them were like one mind, almost.

She could feel Izzie's Jasper energy and how exhausted her friend was because of it. She could feel the lack of control, the dark spots that she had picked up in Izzie's aura. It wasn't only what it looked like, but Izzie felt the holes in her existence. It was a revelation to Alison how strong her friend was to have dealt with this.

The three students looked at each other, each of them nearly drowning in the power that was swirling faster through each of them. It overwhelmed their emotions.

Alison gritted her teeth and shouted to Izzie. "Do you see anything familiar? Are any of these memories yours?"

"Hey!" Horace shouted, walking rapidly toward them. The three teenagers let go, exhausted. Izzie tucked the spell into her pocket quickly and clasped her hands in front of her. The power still hummed in the air around them, but there was no light anymore.

"What did you do?" Horace skidded to a halt in front of them. "What was that magic? That light? I could see it clear over at the barn. Is everybody okay?"

The three teenagers looked at one another. They didn't answer, didn't even have time to decide if they were going to or not when a short figure appeared from the trees.

"Did we conjure something?" Izzie watched as the short figure came closer. The first thing that came into view was her fiery-red hair teased into a carefully arranged bouffant on the top of her head and sprayed until it looked bullet-proof. She wore a team jersey that read Dunk the Donuts over a donut shaped like a basketball. She walked like she had every right to be there as she sucked on a cigarette and blew a puff of smoke into the darkness.

Estelle walked to the three teenagers and blew a smoke ring, a perfect 'o' in their direction. She eyed Horace and the three kids. They were all filled with so much magic that the atmosphere practically hummed with it.

"You were right, nephew." Estelle took another drag of her cigarette. "It's time I showed up. Austin's a little hot this time of year, anyway." She blew out the smoke, her face momentarily disappearing in the haze.

"Hello, Aunt Estelle," Horace said, calmly.

Estelle watched the teenagers. A silver thread appeared between the students, connecting each of them, the magic pulsing back and forth between them.

She put her hand on Izzie's shoulder and got a taste of the magic. "Woooweee! That's a Texas sized serving. What have you been up to, child?" She looked the girl in the eyes, noting how they glowed. "That's right, not my first rodeo. Thought I could retire, mind my little bar, but no... So much magic. Can't even hide it from me, can you? I see everything," she said, narrowing her eyes, the glowing cigarette bouncing between her teeth.

Alison, Izzie, and Tanner were still completely connected. They were in over their heads with magic they didn't understand, but they had done the spell correctly. By some miracle, they had all survived, and it was successful. And yet...

"It should have worked." Izzie took measured breaths, not wanting her friends to feel her sorrow, but it was too late.

Alison could feel the older woman's energy, and see it

JUDITH BERENS

swirl around the tiny Texan. It felt different than anything she had felt before. It wasn't dark, not at all. But it wasn't light, either, not Oriceran. And it wasn't human at all. Humans had no magic. This was something... alien. "Brownstone! That's where I've felt it before."

The moment she thought it, the same thought floated to Izzie and Tanner. They experienced the same other worldly energy, but the information only confused them.

The emotions and thoughts still flowing between them was jarring.

Alison gasped, trying to right herself under the strange sense of connection to the others and magic and the joy and trauma of past memories. She focused instead on Estelle, hoping it would distract her. Estelle was usually good for that purpose.

There was no magical trail that led behind Estelle because the bar owner had no magic of her own, but the energy was definitely there. She was calm, exuding a light blue soul energy, and Horace mirrored that calm. Alison looked at Horace, who shrugged and gave her a wink.

"What? If you're like my dad, then you're an... Is that possible? But you're our Horace!"

"Anything in this world is possible, honey. You're a Drow. You should know that by now. That's Magical Lesson number one," said Estelle, the ash on the end of her cigarette growing longer. "Since you've already stepped in it, pay attention. You've been given a gift very few ever know. Dig into the experience because chances are it will never come again. For just a moment in time, you know what it's like to try on someone else's life."

It was true; the three friends could sense what Alison

sensed, now. For the first time, Izzie looked at the world through her friend's eyes, seeing auras and magic instead of faces. Tanner saw it as well, and it was beautiful and terrifying all at once. He gaped as he looked at everything, feeling the power as well as seeing it like brushstrokes of color. In the darkness, the colors were bright and beautiful —jewel tones in the night. He wondered if it would be the same during the day.

Alison and Tanner could sense the strength of Izzie's Jasper power, like an engine always revving, waiting for a purpose. Tanner's quiet command of spells soothed Izzie's jangled nerves. The different paths merged, blending together and washing over them.

Tanner looked around at the soul colors, getting lost in the information.

"Don't let your mouth hang open like that, son. Catching flies is all it's good for." Estelle blew another cloud of smoke at the students.

Tanner snapped his mouth shut as Estelle puffed on her cigarette.

"I think you best get back to your dorms, now," Estelle said in her Texas accent. She spoke with the cigarette bobbing between her lips.

"Best listen to my aunt. She doesn't generally take to back talk very well," said Horace.

"And don't you go and tell the rest of them, either. It's better if we keep this to ourselves, for now." Estelle blew out a steady stream of smoke, eyeing the kids.

The three teenagers nodded, lightheaded from the flow of energy through their system.

"Our secret to keep," said Alison, staring at Estelle.

JUDITH BERENS

"Blink, honey."

Horace let out a chuckle.

"I know you're going to look for those answers, Miss Alison. You remind me of a little lady I used to watch over back in Austin. It's a good quality to be sure." She took another drag. "But it could get you killed too. Nobody wants that. Keep a watchful eye."

The teenagers looked at each other. Someone was on their side now. They were in the middle of magic they didn't understand, but at least they weren't alone. The three were still gaping at Estelle, wondering about her background.

"Don't you stand there staring. It's rude. Like you've never seen a foreigner before—the three of you just worked up magic that connected you all, and you think I'm strange. I claim Texas as my resting place, that's all you need to know."

Alison took a chance. "And before that?"

"You don't need to know that." Estelle blew a perfect 'o' of smoke. "You have too much on your plates already." She squinted through the smoke at Alison. "But you have a gift, girl." She looked Alison up and down. "A real gift. Go on. Get back to your rooms. Don't make me say it again."

Izzie watched the interaction between Estelle and her friends. She could feel their reactions, but she stayed quiet through all of it. She couldn't place it, but something about Estelle felt familiar.

As they walked away, the others felt it, too. They didn't know what to make of it either, but sharing emotions meant everyone felt what they were all thinking, feeling, and experiencing. It was sharing the burdens and joys, and even though the sensation was strange and didn't allow any of them to hide something from the others, for the first time, Izzie didn't feel like she was alone.

Estelle watched the teenagers enter the school. She waited until they had enough time to walk up the stairs toward their dorms before she set out in the same direction.

"Look after Izzie, Horace. Make sure nothing happens to her. Save me a nice shot of whiskey. I'll be back. I want a few words with Mara Berens. This was *not* part of the deal."

Estelle walked through the damp grass, straight into the main building. It was dark and quiet with everyone asleep in the dorms on the upper floors. She was attuned to the layers of magic performed on the grounds, sticking to the walls and floor. "This is a damn fine school, but there's too much tragedy here to suit me."

She lit a fresh cigarette from the nub of another and dragged on it before stepping through the doors. She looked up, eyeing the sprinklers overhead. "Screw it. I dare you to rain on my parade." She walked across the lobby floors, blowing smoke rings for good measure. No one told Estelle what to do.

She headed toward Mara's cottage.

The old manor hadn't changed one bit. "Need a plant or two to put in the hallway. Finally put in a smoking section." She snorted with laughter, rounding the building.

As she neared Mara's quarters, she heard loud arguing. Estelle slowed when she recognized the voices.

Mara stood on one side of her living room, her robe tightened around her waist, and her hair pulled back in a loose ponytail. Xander Powell was standing on the other side of the room, leaning forward, a vein bulging on his temple, clenching his fists at his side. She was glad his wand was in his pocket. He was barely containing his rage.

"Why didn't you tell me?" Powell said, his voice sharp. "I taught her for *three years*, watched her develop, and you didn't tell me once who she really is. You had no right." He was practically shouting.

"Surely you understand that I couldn't do that and keep her safe." Mara shook her head. "Even you couldn't keep her safe."

"But it's me, Mara. You don't think I'm the problem, do you? I gave up dark magic a long time ago. You know that." Xander's frustration was growing. He threw a glass paper weight instantly regretting it and calling it back, catching it easily in his hand. "You of all people know what I gave up... My own daughter!"

"Eireka," whispered Mara.

"She still has no idea, does she?"

"Of course not." Mara turned to the window. "It's what we agreed to."

"I never thought of you as cruel till tonight. You let me get that close to my own flesh and blood and said nothing."

"Izzie was marked. Her parents begged me to say nothing. You didn't see what was chasing them. I swear to you, this wasn't about your past. It was about giving Izzie a future." She looked out toward the edges of the grounds.

"Even now, they're getting closer. I'm afraid I failed in the end, anyway."

"Then tell me what it's about," Xander said. "Because I'd love to know why you thought you could hide my great-granddaughter from me. You made the girl believe she's an orphan."

Mara shook her head. "This whole thing has gotten away from me." She was stuck in a corner, and no matter which way she went about it, she couldn't reel it back in again. Izzie should never have regained those memories on her own. Her magic should not have gotten out of hand. Xander should not have found out. She should have been able to keep her great-granddaughter safe.

"This is insane, even for you," hissed Xander. "How many lives have you harmed?"

"It was only supposed to last till it was safe to give the memories back."

"Damn, you still won't admit it. You got that spell from me. You used dark magic…"

She cut him off, refusing to admit what he was saying. "Not dark magic. Powerful, dangerous, maybe."

"You tore open their minds and robbed them. Does that sound like something the Light Elves came up with? It was a weapon from the old wars."

Mara wrapped her arms around herself. "I would do it all over again if I had to. I wasn't going to let them die."

"Tell me what's going on," Xander demanded.

"They asked me to do it, Xander. How could I say no?"

"It's not the hardest word to say, Mara!"

Mara swept her arms over her head. The lights started blinking throughout the building, the wires sizzling. Just outside the door, Estelle looked around, nodding her head. "About right."

Mara lashed out in pain and anger without thinking, twisting her wrist in the air as a blue light danced out of the palm of her hand, growing spikes as it slithered across the room and pinned Xander's arms to his sides. "Enough! Do you remember the day you chose dark magic over me? I... I remember every single moment." She choked out the words.

Xander struggled against the magical, thorny ropes, tightening around his chest. "It was all I ever knew. You knew that when you met me."

Estelle came into the cottage, shaking her head. "As long as you think somebody else is the problem, there is no solution. You two hardheads are determined not to learn a damn thing."

Estelle snapped her fingers, blowing out a stream of smoke. The blue ropes turned to sand, littering the floor as Xander breathed in, gasping for air.

Mara leaned against the wall, steadying herself. "I don't know what else to say. I'm tired of this, Xander. They were in trouble. Izzie was in trouble. That menace you used to call family was going to find her. What should I have done? Let the dark wizards like your uncle hunt her down when I could have protected her? I did the best I could."

"The best was obviously not good enough," Xander sneered.

Mara shook her head, his words slicing through her like knives.

"He's not right, honey. And you shut that yap before I sew it shut for you. Don't test Texas, sugar. You won't like the results." Estelle pointed a polished red nail at him. "I've thrown bigger and meaner than you out of my bar. Sit the hell down, both of you. Here's how it's gonna go. You're going to stop thinking about yourselves long enough to get through this particular hell. After that, you can go back to peckin each other's eyes out. I'll be back home by then, sipping a cold one on my patio." She perched her small frame on the arm of the sofa.

"Look, I did what I had to do," Mara snapped, ignoring Estelle's warning.

"It doesn't matter what you say to me, Mara. It won't make this better. I had to let Eireka go because everyone said I was too close to the dark arts."

"Knee deep in them. Some of those goons are your old running mates."

"That's not me, now. It's not fair that you're still holding that over my head."

"Do I need to remind you how many times the Silver Griffins took you in for questioning?" Mara asked.

"Yes, as a suspect, only. I know that. But nothing ever came of it. I have never been to Trevilsom Prison. I'm still a free man, and I've changed. You know I have. You're letting me teach at the school, so you know I'm not a danger to anyone anymore. You had no right to leave me out of any decisions. Not now."

Mara could feel his anger. As if Xander wanted to emphasize it, he clapped his hands, sending waves of energy across the desk to her, letting her feel how upset he was without coming one step closer. The anger rattled across the room, shaking the furniture, rattling the windowpanes, and pushing over books on the shelf.

"Oh, for the love of..." Estelle held on to the edge of the couch.

"A temper tantrum isn't going to help things," Mara said in a cold voice.

Xander laughed bitterly. "Patronize me, Mara. Go on."

Mara shook her head. This was just getting worse and worse. "Maybe Estelle is right."

"When have I ever been wrong?"

Slowly, Xander gained control of his temper. He took a deep breath and let it out slowly.

"She's in danger, isn't she?" he asked softly.

Mara nodded.

"Then it means her mother is in danger."

Mara nodded again. Sadness mixed with her anger, pulling her apart as it had been doing for some time. She was a tough woman, but this was getting impossible to bear, and Xander had been there for her once. He had seen her laugh, held her when she cried, but his darkness had been like an infection.

Xander grimaced, shaking his head. "I'm not going to stand by and wait for disaster to strike."

"What are you going to do?" Mara was immediately worried. "You can't interfere. We need time to plan our next move."

"You had seventeen years to plan. And I was left out of the loop all this time. Your time just ran out."

Mara shook her head again, walking around the table until she stood in front of Xander.

"She has no idea who you are," she said. "She has no idea who she is!" Her voice was shaking, making the chandelier above them rattle.

"And whose fault is that?" Xander turned away from Mara and rubbed his forehead with his fingertips. "Thanks to you, neither of them know me."

"You're not innocent, Xander. You had a hand in making it necessary. The council made you choose, and you did."

Xander yelled, "That's over, too!" He was shouting in pain, the memories of the past, the regrets of who he used to be twisting a fist in his gut.

Estelle stood up and walked quietly between them. She was small but was known to pack a powerful punch when necessary. "Do I need to send for help?"

Xander had a bad past, and there was no guarantee that his demons would ever leave him alone. But he stopped himself from uttering the spell on his lips.

"God help me, sometimes I still miss you."

The words surprised Mara, catching her off guard.

"What we had was real," he said in a quiet voice.

Mara was a bag of emotions as she tried to hold it all in. She didn't want to show him how much she still cared. That would only complicate things that were by no means as simple as they were now.

"And then it all ended," she said flatly, turning away from Xander. He was too close. Any closer and she wouldn't be able to hold it all back anymore. She didn't want to lose it in front of him, or worse, show him she still cared after all these years.

Xander's expression changed, his body going rigid with the pain the clipped words caused. She was glad he was withdrawing. She was only so strong, and there was only so much she could handle.

JUDITH BERENS

"This is why you're still single," he snapped.

"Really?" Mara said with a sarcastic laugh. "And what's your excuse?"

Xander turned and took three steps away, putting distance between them again. The moment was lost, and he was pissed off. He shook his head.

"That's enough! I'm not keeping your secrets for you anymore. Eireka is going to know I'm her father."

He turned around and stormed to the door.

"That will put Leira and Correk in danger," Mara said.

Xander froze by the door, but he didn't look back.

"They already are," he snarled. "All you did was put it off for a while, making it worse because you never asked for help. Not me, not anyone. It was a crime far darker than anything I ever did." He spun around. "You tossed her aside! Made Izzie believe she was an orphan! Unwanted, unloved..." He rubbed his face with his hands. "Three years, Mara. You stole three years from Leira and Correk where they could have watched their daughter grow. Just like I never had those years with Eireka. You're hurting Izzie with this spell. How can you not see that?"

Mara was close to tears, but she bit them back. "I see it all very clearly."

"End it, Mara," Xander said. "End it, or I will."

Mara shook her head. "Give me until the end of the semester." She got her tears under control, swallowing them down.

"Give me one good reason," Xander said.

"I need to find out how the school was breached. I need to figure out what's happening to her and how to stop it so

130

that they don't find her. If they can get in here and they know she's here, we won't be able to stop them."

Xander scowled and reluctantly nodded.

"Fine," he said. "But not one day more, and I will help you whether you like it or not." He was determined to find out who had caused so much trouble and how he could save his family, even if they didn't know who he was.

———

Estelle sensed the fight was over and got ready to leave.

"Estelle, thank you for taking care of Leira all those years. I never had a chance to say that before," Xander said.

Estelle nodded. "It was my pleasure. She's good people. Now, do you want to tell me what the hell the two of you are thinking? It's time to get your heads out of your asses."

Mara opened her mouth to say something, even mention the smoking inside the main hall...

"Get on with things," Estelle added. "No more losses. Find that student, and let's figure out how the bad element is getting inside these walls."

She took another drag on her cigarette and blew a perfect O.

But Mara closed her mouth instead, saying nothing. It was easier to let it go.

CHAPTER ELEVEN

I t was early February, and Valentine's Day was creeping closer. No other dangers had crossed onto the campus, but the missing student wasn't found, either. The tension had eased only slightly, and everyone avoided the small garden where her roommate had been found, crying out in agony.

The Cardinals were getting ready to play, and the entire school turned out, anxious to have something to cheer. The gnomes stood guard at the back, keeping a watchful eye, the poppies on their hats lending a hand.

Faeries filled the stands at the game. They loved a good Louper game, and ever since the School of Necessary Magic got on their winning streak, they were at every game.

The stands were packed, and the team was set to play Chicago's Collegiate for the Magically Gifted Grizzlies.

"New rules!" shouted the coach over the roar from the stands. "Enhanced spells will be used this game. Teams will be able to see each other and interact within the hunt for the golden disc."

There was a gasp from the stands and Luke and David looked at each other. There had been rumors before about a new spell but nothing concrete.

"We deal with it and work out the rest later," said David, looking out over his team of players. "Right now, we have a game to win."

The team all put their fists into the center, one on top of the other and roared. "One for all, and all for the team!"

When the spell was cast, the team found themselves on the brightly lit streets of Las Vegas. The lights were bright, the pavements filled with tourists and gamblers that moved from one casino or restaurant to the next under the colorful neon. There was no sleep for the visitors in Sin City.

At first, the team was dazzled by the noise and chaos. But Henry shook it off, barking out orders, and they got their heads in the game. They had to think straight if they wanted to win this game.

"Singleness of Purpose!" Wyatt shouted, and the race was on to get to the golden disc first. There were so many casinos and hotels that they might need to work through, and the dazzling lights were blinding and attractive all at the same time. The going was rough, and they weaved through crowds, buildings, over roads, and through alleys, following landmarks.

The Grizzlies were just as serious, and they were talented at the game. "Look!' Ethan pointed out the Grizzlie's team captain in the green jersey. He was a tall Light Elf and was running across the open area near the Veer towers of luxury condos, blowing into his palm. A teardrop shaped, purple light formed, rising in the air hovering for a moment before zipping off in the direction of the Aria Hotel.

David signaled to his defensive line of players to follow. "I've seen plenty of trackers, but that's a new one on me."

The purple light zipped by the wall of water and around the circular driveway, dashing into the lobby full of partying bridesmaids.

Both teams stopped where they were, looking at the clusters of women, either on their phones or talking over each other. All the women were only virtual images, but they looked real and dangerous.

A Grizzlie offensive player tried to run past them, bumping into a woman wearing a black leather bodysuit covered by a sheer black dress to her ankles that hid nothing. "Hey! Come back here and apologize," she demanded. Her friends looked up from their phones like gophers popping their heads out of holes, looking around for the source of trouble. They were quickly on him, hitting him with their phones.

His teammates ran to his defense, muttering apologies as they dragged him away.

"What are you looking at? None of this is for you," barked another woman. The other groups of bridesmaids were getting restless. Wyatt and the rest of the Cardinals pressed themselves against the glass of the Aria, slowly making their way around the lobby.

The purple tracking light was still visible up ahead, making its way down the long, wide hallway between the restaurants and shops.

"This is more dangerous than the Louisiana bayou," whispered Luke, not wanting to attract attention.

The Grizzlies finally rescued their teammate, but he had turned an ankle and was out of the game, disappearing from the virtual setting. He found himself standing back on his own home field as a rescue crew ran in and helped him to the sidelines.

The Cardinals were ahead, chasing the light down the hall and through the Park MGM Hotel, past the luxury shops, just as a group of older gamblers, some of them in motorized scooters, decided to get up and head for the restrooms on the other side of the wide hall. In the middle were rows and rows of slot machines, all making noise. The occasional, "whooooeeee!" added to the din.

An old man with wiry, gray hair, wearing a colorful Hawaiian shirt ran over a Cardinal player's foot. The player shook his foot, waving his wand at it, desperate to keep himself in the game.

He smiled, letting out a deep breath. "Whew!" just as the old man backed up, running him over and knocking him down. His image dissolved, and he found himself back on the home playing field.

Just as Ethan was about to clear the gamblers, a woman hit the jackpot, letting out a scream as the numbers spun, and attracting other gamblers who changed course, headed straight at Ethan.

"Go with the flow!" yelled David, signaling to him to move with the virtual gamblers and break out when he got closer to the edge again.

It worked, pushing Ethan out near the top, just in front of a bronze coin that suddenly appeared. An advantage. He reached out, passing his hand through it, and the scenery faded, replaced by the wide-open pavilion in front of the nearby arena. The purple light was just ahead, disappearing inside. Overhead, the giant marquee read, 'Reunion tour with Jackie Venson.'

The Cardinals kept running, hurdling security and picking up speed as the guards gave chase. The Grizzlies were right on their heels. A few gamblers shook their fists at them, but all of them had passed the first hurdles.

Inside the stadium, the ball of light seemed lost, bouncing down different areas, growing fainter. Something was blocking the signal.

Luke turned around and saw the same Light Elf making different hand gestures, tamping down the tracker. No more free help.

They must be near the gold disc.

Wyatt let his pupils separate, scanning in four different directions as he faded into the background, the scales of his skin flipping over, again and again. It was their game plan.

He made his way closer to the Grizzlies as David and the others broke into smaller groups, taking the lower tiers first. The Grizzlies made their way to the stage as a team, turning over the equipment as they searched for the disc.

Henry looked up toward the sky boxes, talking to Luke, the only other shifter on the field, without having to say a word. "Wolf instinct says it's up there. What do you say?"

"I say, I trust my pack. Let's go."

They took the long flight of stairs two at a time, their muscles straining near the top as two wizards from the Grizzlies gave chase.

Luke could feel the pull of the familiar magic, the last clue that they were close to the prize. The only problem was so could the two players behind them. One of them caught up to Henry, taking him down to the ground in a regulation tackle.

Luke barely had time to look back and see Henry cry out, his arm outstretched, upending a Grizzlie as they both faded and disappeared. He was only feet ahead of the other Grizzlie.

"Keep going!" Wyatt was suddenly right next to him, becoming partially visible. He turned and held off the other player, leaving the way open for Luke as he took the last steps and ran through the doors, not even thinking. The energy was stronger to the right, around the curve. Other players were swarming in from the other end. It was going to be a fight to the end.

Luke took a chance and shifted in mid-stride, dropping to all four as a large wolf with his teeth bared. It worked. The other players hesitated just long enough, and he was able to make his way into the luxury box, shifting back into human form just in time to grab the gold disc, bouncing under the glass.

"What the fuuuuu…" gasped Wyatt, as he ran into the room and witnessed Luke's rapid transformation. "I didn't even know you could do that!"

"Me either," said Luke, breathing hard and holding the disc high over his head, a grin across his face.

They had barely made it out against the Grizzlies. It was too close—they nearly lost.

When the spell finally ended, they all stood on the field,

chests burning, breathing hard. The crowd of spectators cheered wildly.

Wyatt clapped Luke on the back.

"Well played, bro," he said.

"You too."

The team was relieved about the win, but they were humbled, too. They had nearly lost.

"We need to work harder," David said, making his way over from the sidelines.

Luke wondered if he was still a little distracted.

"Let's take the win for now," said Wyatt, already making his way over to the cheering spectators. The other team had already disappeared back to their own home field.

A bee landed on Luke's arm and stung him. Luke reached out to grab it, but it flew away, leaving behind an instant welt.

"Dammit," Luke cursed. Ethan could have sworn he saw something shiny on it. "Biotech," he whispered. Too late, the bee got away before he had proof.

After the game, Luke walked to the infirmary. He hid around the corner, waiting until the matron turned her back before he slipped through. He was light on his feet, using his shifter instincts to muffle his steps and slipping into Peter's room. Since Izzie was feeling better, the other bed was empty again.

Peter's face lit up when he saw Luke.

"You're not supposed to be in here."

"Neither are you," Luke said grimly. He sat down. "I'm so sorry you are."

Peter shook his head. "Not your fault. It was my choice. How could you have known?"

Luke pulled up his shoulders. He still felt bad.

"I hear you were the team hero today! Way to go, bro!"

"Lucky move. I tried it a few times over Christmas break. Wasn't sure it would work…"

"Till it did," said Peter, holding up his hand for a high-five.

"That girl, Lisa is still missing."

"Yeah, the nurses told me, and that's about it. Is Izzie okay?"

"Seems to be. I'm keeping an eye on her.

"What are we going to do?" Peter asked.

Luke shook his head. "First, you need to get out of here. Class is not the same without you. Can't they try some healing spell on you?"

"They did, why do you think I'm doing so well? Must have been some kind of magic involved, too. I don't know. Maybe the nurses just want the company." He smiled and pointed at the red welt on Luke's arm. "What is that?"

Luke ran his fingers over it. "Bee," he said. "Little prick." He laughed at his own joke.

Valentine's Day had finally arrived, and the school was decorated in red and white. Magical pink hearts bobbed in and out of the twinkling white lights, and there were red and white flowers being sold in the dining hall. Professor Fowler cast a spell over a close cousin of snapdragons grown on Oriceran, creating a sweet-smelling pink fog that blew around intermittently, rising toward the ceiling and creating unexpected clouds. It gave the effect of a sweet-smelling, romantic sky.

David passed down the hall on the first floor with most of the classrooms, right by the juniors' lockers. He found the one marked 325 and looked around to see if Claire was anywhere in sight. He grinned, despite his overwhelming need to get away before his teammates saw him enchanting the card even as he pushed it through an opening at the top of her locker. Others in the hall were doing the same thing. Valentine's Day at the School of Necessary Magic was in full swing.

Professor Powell saw Alison Brownstone coming down the hall, and he grimaced and changed direction. She saw him just as he turned a corner. She still had no explanation, but Izzie convinced her to let it go for now. They'd keep an eye on him in the meantime, but Alison's bounty hunter skills could be put to better use. Like finding who took Lisa.

Alison reached her locker, and she found a card from Tanner, surprised at her relief. She smiled as she read it, running her hands over the paper as the letters turned to Braille. He had found someone to put a library spell on the card the same way Mara had done for her schoolbooks. She loved it.

Luke carried a bouquet to the dorm where he surprised Izzie just coming out of the door.

"Perfect timing." She smiled.

"Happy Valentine's Day, beautiful," he said. She smiled and pulled into him for a lingering kiss. She loved it when he was romantic, and when things were sweet amidst the chaos.

"You know I'm here, right?" Luke said. "No matter what. I'll always be by your side."

Izzie nodded. "I get it, and it means more to me than I can sometimes say. But we did a spell that was wonderful and powerful and blew my mind but didn't put my memory back together again. Not enough, anyway. Never mind, it's Valentine's Day. Do I have to think about that today?"

The dance was only a few weeks away. Spring was creeping in, and daffodils were already pushing through the ground, braving a late frost to bring the dreary countryside a bit of color.

The other girls in Izzie's dorm room came piling out, all talking at once. Emma and Aya were whispering to each other, laughing. All the chatter was about the dance.

"Do you guys think it's right that we have a dance while Lisa is still missing?" asked Emma. "And what if it happens again?" She dug her hands deeper into her pockets.

Kathleen breathed in the crisp morning air. "You can't live waiting for the next bad thing. It would be all we would do. I have a theory."

"Lay it on us," said Ethan.

"You want to be happy? Live as if a solution is just

around the bend and seek it out, despite any evidence to the contrary. It's my new plan."

"Crazy, but I like it," said Tanner.

"I'm tired of worrying. It's become constant. Does that make me a cold witch?"

"No, a cold Light Elf, maybe," snickered Peter. He was finally well enough to get back to classes.

"Look, there goes another one." Alison pointed in the direction of the circular driveway.

Since Lisa's disappearance, a few parents a week had come to pull their kids from school, fearing for their safety. Fear was running things, and it was understandable.

"Can't blame them." Aya's parents had come, too. But the young witch had refused to leave.

"It's scary, okay, beyond scary," said Izzie. "And maybe the dance isn't the right thing to do. But we can't just live in fear of what happened."

"Aren't we training for times like these?" Alison ducked her chin, smiling. "That solid basement wall… I still say it holds the answer to something."

"Future bounty hunter, weighing in," said Luke.

"We all took turns throwing magic at it. Nothing happened."

"We need to tell a professor."

"Not yet," said Alison. "Not till we know who's on what side."

"I can't believe any of them are on the dark families' side." Izzie glanced over her shoulder to make sure no one could hear them.

"I think we can do this. Solve it, I mean, if we stick together, and share clues." Emma waved her hands. "No, really! Think about it. We raised a dragon—we can do anything."

"Dorvu kind of raised himself, but I hear you. We're young. We're talented, and we're too stupid to know when we're defeated, plus we're good at following spells. Why not?" Ethan shrugged. "Let's do it. All for one?"

"And one for all," they shouted in unison, wrapping their arms around each other.

CHAPTER TWELVE

The dining hall was filled with students, and spirits were running high. Even the pixies were getting in the spirit, wearing pink aprons.

The Cardinals had won another Louper match and were ranked near the top of the league. It felt great to know they were the school that every other magical high school was talking about all over the country. Luke was even getting in extra practice, honing his instincts.

Mara went back to the kitchen, swinging open the door. "Louise," she called. She was practically in a good mood despite Xander's scowl, the parents pulling out students, and the encroaching dark wizards and witches on the school grounds. "Can you make something special for lunch today?"

"They get whatever they want. Isn't every day special?" Louise's wings beat rapidly as she hovered by the refrigerator door.

"You know what I mean, don't bust my chops."

Louise stared at her, finally shrugging. "Fine, I'll bust out the good cheese with the macaroni. That can magically appear on their tables."

"It's all I ask." Mara let go of the swinging kitchen door and looked at all the students; their heads bent near each other. Even Izzie was wearing a smile. "Have to take the good moments where I can." She couldn't shake the feeling that something bad was getting closer, and there was no way to stop it. "No. No, not doing that. What's the point of being magical if we can't stop it?"

The hall was the only place not decorated for the holiday. Instead, it was festooned with the school colors, and some of the witches had created a magical hologram that played a reel of the team's highlights from the season on a continuous loop. Mara waved her arm to silence it finally. A moan went up from the cheer squad. "Know when to quit, girls. It comes in handy."

Luke and David, and the rest of the Cardinals were the center of attention on campus, and they loved it.

While the school celebrated, Jason Parker stood to the side, wanting to join in. He drank his soda and laughed at jokes, all the while moving slowly toward the door. He was half disappointed no one noticed his exit. *Maybe, just once. That would have made a difference.*

He slipped down the hall, looking over his shoulder once or twice and focused on his magic to ensure he wasn't being followed. He argued with himself the entire way, but at the same time, wouldn't change his mind. It was too late anyway. Things had gone too far.

Using a spell he had learned in interdimensional class,

he bent the light, making himself unseen. He made his way to a secluded part of the grounds.

He checked one more time to make sure he was alone before he waved his wand and created a magical, black crow that stood out against the blue sky. The crow flew off, past the glamours and the school grounds to tell his contact he was there.

Jason waved his wand in a series of figure eights, repeating the spell he was recently taught and vanished in an inky, black puff of smoke.

He materialized in the forest beyond the school grounds. The dark wizard he was there to meet was leaning against a tree, waiting. As soon as Jason appeared, the wizard moved quickly, never changing his stony expression as he shoved Jason against a tree. His bony arm was up against the teenager's throat, and he pointed a dirty finger into his face.

"You're not doing enough," he said in a gravelly voice, made worse from scarring leftover from a long-ago battle. "Things need to move faster."

"I'm...I'm doing what I can," Jason stuttered. He was always working so hard at sounding smooth, but panic was rising in his throat, even as the wizard dug a fingernail into his chest.

But Jason's conscience was bothering him. "Are you the one that took Lisa? Is she okay? This wasn't part of the deal."

The man shook his head and laughed in Jason's face, pressing down harder on his throat till Jason coughed and struggled, trying to get out his wand.

"The girl is no longer a problem," the wizard sneered.

Jason could smell whiskey on his hot breath too close to his face. "If you don't find a way to tear down the glamours and the magical wards and detection spells, you'll be next."

"What did you do to her?" Jason felt his knees give way, and the wizard let him crumple at the base of the tree.

"You'll find out soon enough, boy. By the way, Daddy says hello," he snickered.

Jason was finally released and stumbled through the woods back to the campus. He was too shaken to get the words out and send himself back to the grounds.

It was late, and the celebrations were over, a sliver of moon hanging over the trees.

He wound his way past the quiet barns and to the school. He looked up at the windows, imagining everyone asleep in their beds.

"One friend," he whispered. "One real friend would be my wish." He hung his head. It was too late. There was no longer any way out.

Jason's hands trembled, and he shoved them into his pockets, trying to work himself into feeling angry, but it was too hard. All he could feel was fear, wondering what was coming. "Tell no one." He shook his head. "They will never understand."

He opened the door to the entryway, doing his best to shut it without a sound. A bee landed on his shoulder, but he brushed it away. Another and then another came back, building into a small swarm, buzzing around his head before flying into the open door and up the stairs.

"Oh no!"

Nothing was working out the way he wanted.

CHAPTER THIRTEEN

Time seemed to pass slowly for the professors since Lisa's disappearance. The entire staff at the school was on edge. Annabelle Grant was startled in the early morning one day and had temporarily turned one of the faeries who worked in the gardens into a statue. The faerie forgave her, but it was suggested that all wands be kept in pockets, for now.

Mara Berens wasn't sure if that was a good idea or not. She knew something was lurking out there.

She stood at her bedroom window, still wearing her robe, looking out over the carefully tended grounds. It was still early—the sun had barely risen over the horizon, casting yellow rays over the Charlottesville countryside. The landscape was slowly changing from cold and gray to warm and colorful.

But Mara didn't see any of the beauty. She stood in a perfectly decorated room, but she was somewhere else. Her eyes roamed the gentle sloping of the land, hoping beyond hope that Lisa would walk out of the trees unharmed. She wanted to will it into existence, straining her eyes, waiting.

"Has to be a solution. There just has to be. You got out of the world in between, surely..." It had been several weeks since the girl's disappearance, and she was nowhere to be found. Her disappearance hung over the school like a cloud. The headmistress felt personally responsible for it. Lisa had been placed under her care, just like every other student.

She took a deep breath and let it out with a shudder.

Lisa's roommate, Sophie, wasn't doing very well, either. She was still traumatized from the spell that was placed on her and forced terrible images into her mind. Lisa's absence only added to her distress. Mara had spoken with her parents about letting the girl take a semester off, but the witch and wizard said they were going to be traveling, and it was best if she stayed in school.

Mara had held the phone away from her face for a moment to repeat every swear word she knew under her breath, before putting the phone back.

"I understand, completely. We'll do our best." She hung up and shook her head. "Never ceases to surprise me."

A knock on Mara's door snapped her out of her second bout of swearing. She walked over and opened it, finding Annabelle Grant on her threshold.

The young professor looked like she was working up the nerve to say something, folding and unfolding her arms across her chest. She was wearing faded jeans and a dark purple sweater with brown suede loafers. Her long brown hair was braided loosely with strands escaping over her shoulders, and her eyes were serious.

"Is everything okay?" Mara peeked out, looking in both directions for trouble.

"There's nothing out there. Nothing new has happened. I haven't changed a student into a toad. But this disappearance is really bugging me. We need more of a plan. Do something, be proactive. Isn't there something else we can be doing to find the girl?"

"I'm open to any suggestions." Mara stepped to the side, letting Annabelle into her private quarters.

"Coffee?" Mara offered as Annabelle sat down in the small sitting area. Mara's favorite deck of Oriceran playing cards sat on the end table next to a red velvet chair.

"No, thank you. I've already had two cups." She took a deep breath and let it out with a resolve, rubbing her hands together. "Look, I'm... I'm here to do something. Put me to work."

"I've called in bounty hunters," Mara said. "They should arrive a little later."

"Bounty hunters?" Annabelle asked.

Mara nodded and perched on the edge of the armchair. "The bounty hunters are good at what they do. I have hope they'll find Lisa, maybe even catch who's done this. Put an end to their plots and schemes."

Annabelle nodded, brushing a strand of dark brown hair out of her face.

"I just keep wondering how it's possible that she vanished like that, with no sign of a security breach that we could pick up and no sign of her on campus. She's not invisible. Did they have a way out of here none of us noticed? Advanced technology? A deal with the world in between?"

Mara winced but did her best to hide it. *That dreaded place.* "That's what I'm hoping the bounty hunters can clear up for us. If anything, they can find where they managed to sneak the girl out of here."

"Do you think it will work?"

Mara took a deep breath. "I believe it has to."

They sat together in silence for a while till Annabelle reached out and took Mara's hand.

"How are you holding up?"

Mara looked up surprised. "I'm fine."

"Really? I don't know if you heard, but I tried to add to the garden decorations." Annabelle gave a tight smile.

"I did, and it took some convincing to get the faeries not to form their own union. I told them that would not prevent the stray spell going awry at a high school full of hormonal magicals, and this was carefully explained when they took the job."

"I owe them something. Maybe some of the peonies they love."

"That would be a good idea."

"That way I won't have to worry about a vine growing up my ankle."

Mara smiled despite the long days that had passed since Sophie had been found screaming in the courtyard.

Annabelle saw the pain flash across her face. "You couldn't have stopped this."

"Maybe not," Mara said. "But we've had too many incidents lately. Peter hasn't been out of the infirmary long, and that darkness that beat him up is still somehow causing damage."

"He should not have gone out on his own to investigate."

Mara nodded. "You're right. He shouldn't have. But he was looking for something, something we had all shrugged off as unimportant. And *he* found it, a student."

"He'll make a great journalist someday."

"If he's going to grow into an old journalist, he has to get better at defending himself. Thank goodness he's learning how to speed up his reaction to dark magic here at school."

"They wouldn't have hurt him like that if he hadn't been onto something important."

"I wasn't able to stop that from happening, either. And Izzie is struggling, too."

"Don't do this to yourself," Annabelle said. "You have held this school together and defended our grounds more than once. If you weren't here, then none of the parents would have let their children stay. It's a testament to your skill and badass courage."

"Badassery has gotten me into more trouble than out."

"I hear stories." Annabelle smiled. "Mind if I make us some tea? Don't get up. I know where it is in your cupboard."

"In the end, I'm responsible. The wand stops here."

"We work best when we work as a team. Let all of us help you solve this." Annabelle waved her wand over the teapot, filling it with steaming mint tea. She carried a tray with two cups over to the coffee table.

Mara took a cup of tea from Annabelle. *I can't tell her*

everything. Especially not about Izzie's magic. And something happened with Alison, too. Mara couldn't quite put her finger on it, but every time she passed the two girls she could feel it. *Something was... different.*

"Anything you can do to help the students have as normal a semester as possible, that's helpful. In the meantime, we need to find out how they're getting in and out of the grounds. I've asked the gnomes to search the old archives for any plans from the property that show something we've missed. It's possible that over the years Turner Underwood built hidden entrances or tunnels."

"That magic can't detect? Unlikely."

"True, but it is possible. I have to get dressed." Mara stood up, signaling it was time for Annabelle to go. "Can we finish our tea another time? The bounty hunters will be here shortly."

Annabelle set down her cup. "Of course, I have to create a lesson plan on the oldest known kemana in Portugal to get ready for the day. Still a thriving community, but the only place with gnomes who never come out of the kemana. Like their cousins on Oriceran who live in the mountains."

Mara let her out of her private quarters, and Annabelle made her way through the corridors and out of the school building to her own cottage.

Bees followed her as she walked, swatting at them. She pulled out her wand just as a faerie flew by, gasping and turning tail. "One time! I changed someone to stone one time! And it was just for a minute, maybe less," she called after the faerie, but she didn't return. "Maybe donuts would make it better. Who doesn't like donuts?" She raised her wand, but the bees were already gone. "Next time. We don't need any more accidents."

———

Mara stood on the stone steps, just in front of the tall mahogany doors that led into the main hall. She was waiting for the bounty hunters to come up the long driveway. The perimeter spells had shuddered when they had entered, announcing their arrival.

Their car was a modern, sleek black sedan, completely silent aside from the crunch of gravel under the tires as it parked. Three men emerged—the man who was obviously in charge and his two sidekicks, who looked like identical twins.

"Hello. We're from Obsidian Sanctum," said the man. "We spoke on the phone. I'm Bruce Madden." The company was unusual because they worked with magicals to find preternatural criminals and deal with them according to their transgressions.

Obsidian Sanctum did not advertise their services anywhere. Instead, they relied only on word of mouth, and through the magical community, word had traveled far and wide that Bruce Madden was the one human they could call on in a time of need and get a solution.

"Thank you for coming so quickly, Mr. Madden." Mara held out her hand to shake.

"Call me Bruce, please." He was a tall man, broad in the shoulders, with dark hair and three-day stubble on his chin. He had an air of business— first, last, and only hobby —about him.

"These are my associates, Melvin and Ralph," Bruce said, introducing the twins. "If there is anything or anyone you need found, trust me, we'll find it."

The twins looked like they had been cloned from one another. Large, hooked noses matched in size by their ears sticking straight out on the sides. Light brown hair combed to the side, jeans, shirts, and sneakers - all identical. They even moved in unison, scratching their nose in the same way at the same moment. Mara glanced back to get another look, wondering just how strange this day was going to get.

Mara nodded at the twins. "Follow me. The sooner we get started the better."

"We can take it from here. We got your report. It was very thorough. We have the run of the grounds?" Bruce swept his arm out to the right.

"As long as you don't involve any of the staff or students. If that becomes necessary…" Mara hesitated, holding up her hand. "You tell me first. I'll deal with my own people."

"I get that a lot. You'll learn to trust me. Okay, fair enough. Let's get going, gentlemen."

"Fair enough," said the twins, setting off together on their right foot at the same moment. Mara was doing her best not to stare. "Have to be Light Elves," she muttered.

"Only one quarter. Mostly wizards." Bruce smiled, watching the twins walk away. "Very talented. It's like another sense with them."

"What sense is that? Don't you need to go with them?"

Bruce ignored her question. "Trouble, dark magic. They

can smell it and even have visions. It comes in handy in our line of work."

When the twins finally turned the corner around the building, Bruce climbed the stairs to Mara, leaning in close. She took a step back, frowning. *What now?*

"I don't mean to be a prophet of doom, Ms. Berens. But it does not look good for your student."

Mara's stomach tightened.

"I have taken the liberty to search the dark webs, and I have an ear to the ground at all times. There is no chatter about your student. Nothing about the disappearance other than the general news that has been spread."

"What does that mean?" Mara was growing more and more agitated.

"It means that whoever did this was incredibly skilled, so skilled that they managed never to be spotted—which is hard with a screaming teenager or even a limp body. It could mean that she is still on campus."

Mara closed her eyes for a moment when Bruce mentioned a limp body. Limp, not dead. He had not said dead. She took a deep breath.

"We have searched the campus several times," Mara said. "I don't think she's here."

Bruce nodded. "My associates will find something if there is anything to be found. They have access to magic I have never seen, and spells that have not been used in centuries. They're a wonder to behold."

"I don't suppose I want to know how they came across these spells?"

"Wise woman. I've always suspected it had something to do with busting up the Silver Griffins vault all those years ago. But I don't like to ask things if I'm going to have to do something about the answer, you know?

Mara nodded. "No visions from the twins?"

"None so far. That's another good sign. Death usually brings a big one, and these guys are great at that."

"I don't care how great these guys are, or if they're some kind of super magicals. All I need is for them to find the girl and find the hole in our security."

"That's why we're here, ma'am. It's a pity something so heinous had to happen here. Nice place you got."

———

Melvin and Ralph moved across the school grounds, walking in lockstep with each other. They were particularly sensitive to elementals, and even though they were identical in every other chilling way, Melvin could only sense magic from the ground, and any disturbances in the earth. Ralph sensed magic in the air and how it shifted, and if it was affected by emotions or spells.

"I don't like it," Melvin said. "Not one bit. There is *nothing* wrong here." Melvin thoughtfully scratched his chin. He leaned down and pulled up a handful of grass, holding it tightly in his hand.

"Or if there is, it's been hidden too well to find." Ralph sniffed the air. "No, nothing."

A bee flew by, briefly buzzing around them, then flying off, away from the building.

They both felt it and looked at each other.

"A man," one said.

"More of a boy, really. On the inside," the other finished.

"That's not good."

"Split up," they said in unison, walking in opposite directions, one with his nose pointed toward the ground, the other with his nose pointed up in the air. Still looking somehow identical.

Melvin walked back toward the main building, sensing the earth under his feet and how many magicals had crossed it recently. He found the trails. The tracks that were nearly wiped away or crossed by another set of prints. "Still doable." He smiled, a growing sense of confidence. "You will not stay hidden from us."

Ralph stood in a hallway on the first floor near the classrooms. He sniffed the air, trying to figure out where to go next, just as the school bell rang, and students poured out the doors all around him. He froze, curious about the magic patterns they created in the air as they moved, going from one class to the next.

One particular student drew his attention with her long grey hair and glasses that left their own magical trail. Her face was even familiar.

Alison was walking with her head down, deep in thought when she walked into Ralph. She looked up just before they made contact, startled, smashing her nose into his arm.

"Sorry, lipstick on your shirt. My bad." The trail of magic behind her was strong, and Ralph wanted to breathe in deeply and feel the energy. His chest puffed up, and he smiled. Drow Princess. He hadn't encountered one for a very, very long time.

Ralph shook his head. "Don't worry about it."

"Who are you?"

"Ralph with Obsidian Sanctum. We're here about the missing girl. My brother is around here somewhere."

Alison narrowed her eyes.

"I'm a bounty hunter," he added.

Alison's face lit up. "That's cool."

"You're familiar I take it. Last name Brownstone?" He could feel her power trembling through her.

Alison startled. "You know my father?"

"Everyone does. I saw you both at the scene of a takedown this past summer. A woman was with you?"

"Uh… mom, kind of…" Alison felt the word roll around in her mouth. Shay Carson as her mom.

"Interesting family you got there. Kind of mom, huh? I get it." Ralph sniffed the air again. "Your dad is a legend. Melvin and I see him as the gold standard."

Alison smiled and nodded. "Yeah, he's the best."

"Are you going to join the family business? I would kill to be on a team with someone as powerful as you are, dramatically speaking, of course."

"I'm thinking about it," Alison admitted.

Ralph nodded. He had run out of words. "More of a man of action. Me and my brother, we don't talk much. No need to."

"Okay, sure, well… I have to get going." Alison jabbed a thumb over her shoulder. "Class. You know, student." She cleared her throat. "Awkward," she muttered.

Ralph nodded and watched her walk away. When she was gone, he walked through the field of energy she had left with his hands held out over the floor. He would not touch her magic without her permission. That was rude. But the close contact alone was enough to make him shiver. "A Brownstone and a Drow Princess. I have to tell Melvin."

Alison walked down the hall to her next class in magical history. The hall was nearly empty. More than half of the students were gone—their parents had pulled them out of school, homeschooling them while they waited for the disappearance to be resolved.

It was strange for the school to be so empty. An eeriness hung in the air as Alison hurried to get to her class.

Professor Hudson was already addressing the class when she walked in.

"I'm sorry I'm late." Alison hurried across the room to take her seat next to Izzie.

"Why so late?" Izzie whispered.

Alison shrugged. "Bounty hunters."

"What?"

"Girls!" Professor Hudson arched an eyebrow, staring right at Alison.

"Is this it?" Hudson asked, looking at the handful of students. "Are you the only ones left?"

The students nodded, looking around.

Hudson sighed. "Maybe the dark families' plot to close the school is actually working. All right, we will soldier on and keep the doors open. Today, we learn the truth behind the story of the Wizard of Oz. Yes, I know, Kathleen, we did the musical. Fact or fiction? Fact, students. Obvious as the nose on your face. It has everything, although I've never seen water take out a witch, thank goodness."

Classes ended early that day, and everyone headed back to the dorms to get ready for the annual Spring Dance. Alison and Izzie had been to the kemana to shop, despite the new restrictions on leaving the grounds.

Alison was wearing a dress with an empire waist made of soft, flowing linen that moved around her legs as she walked. Izzie wore a strapless dress that traced her body to her knees before it flared out. Aya was in a bright, yellow silk dress, and Jennifer was wearing a little black dress with a bright red belt that went well with her red curls. Kathleen and Emma both wore white—Emma's with a lace overlay. Alison's grey hair hung in curls over her shoulders.

"I'm glad they didn't cancel the dance."

"Me too. It's like we've all been in suspended animation waiting for the mystery to be solved."

"We can take one night off."

"Come on. Our dates are waiting. Let's get to the dance."

"We look gooood."

They laughed and grabbed each other's hands, walking out of their dorm room.

When they walked into the dining room, they gasped at

the transformation. The dining room was transformed for the dance.

The whole room was decorated with flowers everywhere—wreaths of pink rose buds hung on the doors, lilies in vases decorated every flat surface, and Queen Anne's lace hung from the lights, refracting the light. Ivy crawled up the walls, colored pinpoints of light hanging on the leaves.

"Everything looks so magical," gasped Aya.

"In the truest sense of the word." Kathleen spun around, looking at all the decorations.

The tables were covered with white linen tablecloths. An ice sculpture of a pixie was in the middle of the table near the kitchen.

Jennifer laughed. "Inside job from the pixies, definitely."

"This is perfect," Izzie said, grinning.

Tanner and Luke stepped forward to escort their girlfriends into the transformed hall. Tanner was wearing a dark blue suit with a tie in the school colors.

Ethan put out his arm for Aya as Peter stepped forward to say hello to Emma.

"You clean up well," Izzie said to Luke. He was dressed in a pale grey suit and blue tie.

"Never as well as you do," Luke said, and Izzie felt her cheeks warm. Luke dipped his head down to press his lips against hers.

They walked to their table, surrounded by their friends. Alison noticed Professor Powell lurking near the stage. She elbowed Izzie. "We should take turns keeping an eye on him."

"Not tonight, remember? One day off, bounty hunter."

Alison shrugged but looked back one more time.

As the friends took their seats, appetizers of a cold cucumber-and-avocado soup with cream appeared.

"I'm glad I didn't know what it was before I tasted it. I actually like it!" said Ethan.

The entrée consisted of roast duck in red wine sauce on a bed of wild rice, accompanied by steamed vegetables.

"I would never have thought I would say this about vegetables," said Peter, "but I want this every day for the rest of my life."

Luke laughed. "You'd get sick of it."

"Not this." Ethan's mouth was full, one cheek bulging out. "Why can't we eat like this every day?"

"Because then it wouldn't be special," Izzie said.

Ethan shook his head, swallowed, and shoveled another fork load into his mouth. "Messed-up logic. Investigate this next, Peter."

For dessert, there was a light chocolate mousse with spun-sugar that glowed and twinkled with the constellations. Alison looked up at the ceiling overhead where the spell was enchanting the old plaster to look like the evening sky. The stars matched.

The students ate until they couldn't eat anymore.

Once the plates were cleared, the headmistress appeared on the small stage at the front of the room. She wore a form-fitting, navy-blue dress and was smiling for a change.

"Maybe she took a night off too," whispered Izzie.

The students watched her as she walked to the front of the stage.

"Having fun?" she asked, holding out her arms.

The students cheered, some getting to their feet.

She nodded with a chuckle and asked everyone to move away from the tables. Once they did, Mara raised her hands again, moving her fingers in a pattern.

"Transform tabulas in lucem." Some of the tables disappeared while others moved to the sides of the room, creating a dance floor. A band appeared in the corner with older light elves all dressed in black tie. The windows were open to let in the night air, moving the scent of the roses through the room.

The students cheered again and quickly took to the dance floor, laughing, and talking in high-pitched voices.

Mara smiled at her students, glad that they could find a time to enjoy themselves despite the terrible events that kick-started the year. Despite Obsidian Sanctum not finding anything useful.

"Yet," Bruce had said. "It's still early in the game."

"Not to us," Mara had answered. "We need answers now. Mara shook off the disappointing memory and focused on the dance.

Xander Powell had moved to the side of the dining room just under the tall windows, his arms folded over his chest. He watched Izzie dance with Luke, trying to decide if he liked the shifter or not.

Not that he could say or do anything about it.

Izzie saw him staring as she spun under Luke's arm and frowned before she was turned around the other way.

"Why is Professor Powell staring at us?" Izzie whispered to Luke when he twirled her again on the dance floor.

Luke looked up to see Powell staring, arching an eyebrow at him.

"I don't know," he said. "Maybe he's just making sure no one else disappears."

"Or just me. You think he knows something?"

Jason Parker walked by, his head down and his hands in his pockets, but no one noticed. He went to lean against a far wall, his usual smile not in place.

Luke pulled Izzie against him. "No, I don't, and that's fine by me. I don't want you going anywhere." He kissed her, and when he looked up, Powell was glaring at him.

"Okay, that's a little weird. Could be he has a thing about shifters. Not the first."

"I kind of like them."

Luke smiled and kissed her again. "All that matters."

Alison danced by Izzie, moving around the floor with Tanner, looking like she was in seventh heaven. Izzie could feel the euphoria, too. Since they had done that spell, Izzie could feel everything Alison and Tanner felt, and think everything they thought. But tonight, even though Izzie was still very much connected to them, she knew they were in their own little world.

You deserve to be. All of us do.

They had all gone through hardships. Ethan let out a loud whoop, making Aya laugh.

Tanner pulled Alison closer for a kiss and ran his fingertips over her cheek.

"Have I told you that you look stunning tonight?"

Alison blushed and nodded. "Three times, already. And I can hear you inside my head, thinking it."

"So, not nearly enough, then."

Alison smiled, blushing even harder.

Tanner looked around. "This place is really incredible. The students that set it up did a fantastic job. Scarlett may be hard to take at times, but the girl can organize."

The senior students were put in charge of decorating for the dances. It was a challenge for each class to outdo the class before every year, using magic to bring the theme to life. This year's theme was the Oriceran royal garden.

"Yeah, it's the stuff of dreams," Alison said.

Tanner frowned.

"What's wrong?" Alison asked him, although she already knew.

"Don't you think it's a little wrong that we're having fun when Lisa is still missing?" Tanner asked. "We're still in danger, and so much has happened."

Alison shook her head. "What happened is awful, and I worry about Lisa every day. But we deserve to have a good time. We're teenagers with only one year of school till we're out there full time. We deserve to live our lives. Everything will be okay in the end. If it's not okay yet, this can't be the end."

Tanner nodded. "Okay, one night, for you."

The dance was a successful distraction for most. A celebration of life and light – for just one night.

CHAPTER FOURTEEN

Slowly, the days became warmer, and the students traded their coats and leggings for short-sleeve shirts and summer dresses or shorts.

The grass was turning from yellow to green again, and the first tulips were poking their heads out of the soil.

The students spent more of their time outside, often next to one of the many small rivers.

Horace stood by the barn wearing a beekeeper's suit. He held the netted hat under his arm and looked out over the grounds toward the deep woods taking a deep breath. The smell of the approaching summer was in the air. He ran his hand through his red hair, wiping the sweat off his brow with a white handkerchief.

A low roar attracted his attention, and he looked up at Dorvu sailing through the sky, blowing out a trail of frosted air and flying through the center of it to cool off.

A large bumble bee buzzed around Horace's head, and he swatted at it angrily, his momentary good mood shaken.

He had spent the morning trying to get the bees into their own hives by capturing the queen who had to be near the swarm

But Horace couldn't find the queen.

On the game field, located on the other side of the grounds, the Cardinals were gathering. Luke and David looked at each other with a nod. "Let's do this." They pounded padded fists together.

The San Francisco Bay Area Sandpipers, their rivals, appeared at the start of the spell, and the whistle sounded that the Louper match was starting. The stands were filled with students waving signs, *Go Cardinals* and stomping their feet, despite the reminder that the players could no longer see them.

A virtual sign hung off the side of the stands with a picture of Lisa, and a brief description of what she looked like, what she had been wearing, where she was last seen, and who to call to give information. No one really noticed the sign anymore. Months had passed, and there was still no sign of her.

Most had given up and gone back to their routine. Not Alison Brownstone. She was still working clues, but Izzie had begged her to come to the game.

"Look, this is where almost everyone is. See? Even creepy Professor Powell is here. Your best chance to find a clue is right here, cheering with your best friend by your side."

"All right, I'll buy the leap of logic... for now."

"I'll take it."

"There goes more bees. What the hell..." Kathleen covered her head with her purse as the bees flew overhead and kept going.

"They're already gone. Watch the game. It's starting."

The last time the Cardinals played the Sandpipers, they had lost because the Sandpipers had cut corners to get to the gold disc first. The Cardinals weren't going to let it happen again.

"Bring it!" Luke was determined.

The Sandpipers were not going to win again. Luke was sure of that— but he wanted to win fair and square.

"Are we ready for this?" Henry asked the Cardinals all huddled together.

The team raised their fists in the air, cheering.

"Let's take them down!" Luke yelled. His eyes glowed as his wolf energy slid behind them, just beneath his skin. He was more than ready to do this, to get the problems at the school out of his head and go somewhere else, even if it was just a virtual world in a game.

Professor Regency called the warning then finished casting the spell.

The team looked around at the new scenery. They found themselves standing in shifting sand in the desert. Not the usual location for a game. No city streets or deep jungle that could hide the golden disc and their opponents.

There was nothing around them but miles and miles of sand dunes as far as they could see. The sun was hot, and the heat bounced off the sand making it even hotter. Luke held his hand over his eyes against the glare from the virtual sun, looking around. "There has to be a stumbling block here somewhere, an obstacle we have to overcome."

Wyatt easily blended into the sand, making himself

invisible. "What do you think? Are we going to have to walk for miles and miles? That can't be it."

"This makes no sense." Henry scanned the horizon, looking for anything that stood out.

"Let's change it up and stick together this match," Luke said. "We'll figure it out. Something is up, but as long as we stick together, we can do this."

"That shifter logic? Stick to the pack?" Wyatt let the scales along his arm flip over, revealing where he stood.

"Works for me," said David.

"You would say that."

The ground beneath Luke's feet shifted with every step, making it hard to get any momentum. With every step, he had to fight to get his foot out of the sand again. He contemplated shifting into wolf form. It would be easier to cover ground that way.

Before he had a chance to make up his mind and do it, the sand became softer and softer, and the team members rapidly sunk up to their calves.

"What's going on?" David did his best to keep the alarm out of his voice.

Luke looked at the others. "Dammit! Quicksand? This is not right!"

"Did someone play with the spell?"

"Don't fight it!" Luke shouted. But the urge to wriggle free was too strong, and even Luke couldn't keep still, despite telling everyone else not to move.

He sank deeper into the sand until it was up to his waist, feeling the weight against him. The terror was clutching at him as the sand reached higher and higher. When he was buried neck-deep, he held his breath.

For a moment, it flashed through his mind that this might be how the dark families finally took them out—this was just a spell to kill them all.

Not the end... No! Wait, wait a minute. My feet are...

His feet were dangling. The sand gripped his body, but as he sank, his body was shaking loose, and he realized his feet were hanging in mid-air.

Okay, here we go. One foot or one story off the ground. Gotta do it.

Henry, the only other shifter on the team, heard him and sent back a message. *Go for it!*

Luke held his breath and straightened up, sinking faster and suddenly dropped all the way through. He landed on his feet, agile as the wolf inside him, and bent his knees until his fingertips touched cold stone. The others dropped down next to him with yelps and screams.

When they were all together again, he surveyed the area. They were in an underground cave with smooth rock walls and floors. The ceilings were low and rounded, and torches lit the area all around them. The ceiling was a swirling funnel cloud of sand.

"Is everyone okay?" David checked in with his team members. "Anyone hurt?"

"I'm okay."

"All clear."

"Nothing's broken, just a few bruises."

Each team member sounded off with the all clear.

"Let's move out then. We still have a game to win. Keep your eyes open for that disc and any Sandpipers. They have to be nearby."

"Let's split up and look for the exit out of this place."

Luke felt along the walls, looking for any hidden levers or any other tricks in the game. "The challenge is going to be to get out of these underground caves and tunnels and find the treasure before the Sandpipers do."

"Let's go." David waved his team onward. "The quicker we move, the faster we figure this out. Wyatt, you want to go ahead of us and scout it out?"

Wyatt's pupils separated, looking in four different directions, even as the scales along his arms flipped over, blending into the darkness of the cave. "This way, everyone."

They fell in line behind him and headed toward one of the tunnels.

"This is a very funky match," muttered Henry.

"Name of the game. Anywhere is a good start." David led the group into the narrowing tunnel.

"Uh guys, I don't think this is your normal under-ground labyrinth." Ethan covered his head as droplets of water pinged him. As they made contact, they turned into scorpions crawling down his arms. "Eeeeyaaagh!" He swatted as fast as he could, avoiding their stinging tails.

"Cover your heads! Cover your heads!" David lifted his thick jersey over his head.

A droplet of water landed on another senior's shoulder before he could react, and quickly turned into a scorpion, stinging him in the neck. He screamed in pain and disappeared from the game, returning to the home field.

"One down. Stay sharp."

Before long, they reached rushing water that ran parallel to the walkways. Ethan reached down, dipping his hand in the water and brought it to his lips despite Luke's admonitions. "Stop! That could be poisoned!"

"Don't care. Too thirsty." He slurped it up. "Hey, this water is sweet, cold even!"

"You got lucky. We can't afford to lose another player. Get up and come on." Luke growled low, making Ethan's eyes widen.

"I'm going; I'm going."

Wyatt let the scales on his body turn back to their natural dark brown state making him visible again. He held up his hand for everyone to stop.

The sound of rushing water was becoming louder and louder. It echoed along the stone walls like thunder.

They came around the corner and found themselves standing on a precipice above a river. Their path continued on the other side. The water was wild and churning, rushing out of a dark tunnel in the wall on its way to another.

"The only way forward is across the river," yelled David over the noise.

"We can't get over that," Wyatt said.

David shook his head. "We don't have a choice. We can't double back."

"Are you scared?" Ethan asked, taunting Wyatt, who was trying to hide his trembling hands.

"Of course not," Wyatt snapped. "I'm realistic."

"Whatever you want to call it." Ethan gritted his teeth.

Wyatt noticed and slapped Ethan on his back. "We can do it." He shook his head. "Fine!" he yelled.

He rocked back and forth, swinging his arms to build momentum, and ran toward the rushing water. With a cry, he kicked off and lunged himself across the river. His skin blended itself into the color of the rushing water, disappearing halfway across and reappearing as he landed with a thud. He came down hard, stumbled, and fell, rolling on his back.

He stood and dusted himself off. "I made it!" He offered Ethan an I-told-you-so look, even as he breathed a sigh of relief, pumping his fist in the air.

Ethan pulled up his shoulders. "Good man. You did it."

"Time's ticking down. Let's get a move on." Luke got ready to make a run, but Ethan went sprinting past him, letting out a guttural scream.

He jumped, arms wind-milling and landed without a stumble. One more across the obstacle. One step closer to the gold disc. Only one player lost, so far.

One by one, all the team members crossed until only— Henry, David, and Luke were left. David went next, easily making it to the other side. Luke gestured for Henry to go.

Henry was fast enough, but as he kicked off his foot slipped, and he didn't make it all the way across. Instead of landing on the other side, Henry fell into the water close to the edge. "Son of a…"

He grabbed for the rock, but his wet hands were slippery. It didn't help that the undertow was strong, and he was getting battered against the rock as he tried to climb up to safety.

Luke was poised, and about to jump just as Henry was yanked underwater, a look of surprise on his face. A moment later, he bobbed to the surface again, only to be sucked through the hole in the wall, washing him quickly farther downstream away from the rest of the team.

"Shit, shit, shit! What do we do?" Wyatt raised his hands in the air, stomping his feet.

"Keep going. Take the rest of the team with you." Luke shouted across the water to David. "We'll find you." He didn't wait for a response. He jumped into the water feet first and let the current drag him through the opening after Henry. The last thing he saw before being sucked under the same way was the shocked faces of his team members. *All for one...*

For a moment, his head was underwater, and when he tried to come up for air, the rock ceiling stopped him. There was no space above the water—he was in a narrow chute.

But then the rock surrounding him opened up again, and he gasped for air when his head broke through the water.

He found himself still washing downstream at an alarming pace, riding with his head just above the waves.

"Henry!" he shouted, coughing as the water poured into his mouth. He timed the next one and waited until his head was at the highest point. "Henry!"

He heard a faint reply up ahead, but it was too far ahead. The waters were slowing enough that he could start swimming, moving in the direction of the voice.

"Dude!" Henry called, and Luke saw him on the side of the river, sitting on a flat rock where the river created a bank, still breathing heavily.

Luke swam toward the edge and pulled himself out of the water. He sat next to Henry, coughing. His hair and his clothes dripping wet. He was fighting the urge to throw up all the water he swallowed.

"Where are the others?" Henry asked.

"Back there," Luke said, pointing in the direction they had come from. "They're going on. We'll find them. "

"How? This place is a maze."

Luke shook his head. "We'll figure it out. It's a game, after all. They want us to have a fighting chance."

"Barely, it seems."

"But we can't do it sitting down, so come on." Luke pushed himself up and wrung out the worst of the water in his clothes. Henry did the same.

"Which way?" Henry asked.

Luke shook his head. "I have no idea. We'll just have to pick a route and make it happen."

Henry nodded, following Luke back in the direction they had washed down the river. The path was far rockier than what they had followed before, and they soon had to climb over large rocks. A few times, Luke's sneakers slipped on the loose rocks, and he fell, scraping a knee or an elbow.

Henry helped him up, and they kept going.

"Cardinals!" Luke called every now and then, hoping for a reply.

David, Wyatt, Ethan and the rest of the team slowly walked through the tunnels, searching for the gold disc, a way out, and their two missing teammates.

"Well, if it isn't the Cardinals," someone said. They had run straight into the path of the Sandpipers. "Where's the rest of your team?"

"We split up to cover more ground," Wyatt said.

"Did you lose them?"

David shook his head. "No, we're sending them ahead to win while you guys are standing here mocking us."

The Sandpipers looked worried for a moment until the team captain grinned.

"Forget them," he said to his team. They turned around and walked away.

David did a quick count. "They still have their entire team."

"Not for long," said Wyatt. "They won't hold together through all the obstacles."

"We have to find Luke and Henry," Ethan said. "We have to win this thing."

"Then let's get going."

They eventually found them trying to climb up a steep pile of rocks toward the ceiling of a cave, their hands slipping.

"I thought this is how we started this mess. What are you doing?" Wyatt asked behind them.

Luke looked over his shoulder. "Getting out of here."

"Through the ceiling?" Ethan asked.

Luke chuckled and let go, slipping down. Henry followed.

"There's a narrow tunnel up there. We thought it might be the way back to you guys," Luke said.

"Hey, at least we're together," Ethan said. "We ran into the Sandpipers. Same dicks. Let's beat these guys."

"Cardinals!" shouted Henry, holding out his fist. They all held out their fists. "For the team!"

"Okay, enough, we need to get going." Henry set out, leading the way. There was no time to waste.

It wasn't easy to find their way out, but after a few dead ends, two cold swims through the snaking river, and another climb over rough rocks, they saw the treasure. It looked at them like a pot of gold at the end of a cold, hard rainbow plastered against a stone wall. It was a straight run to it over a long distance, using legs that were close to giving out.

"Look," Ethan said, nudging Wyatt and Luke. The Sandpipers appeared on the other side.

"We *have* to get there before they do," Luke said. The Sandpipers were the same distance away as them. It was suddenly a race against time, and who could dig down deeper to find the energy. The team set out at a dead sprint. But it wasn't going to be enough. Luke knew it right away.

"I've got this," Luke said. "Stay on me."

Without waiting for an answer, he shifted into wolf form. The others gaped at him. He shook himself out and bolted forward, his paws better able to grip the surface, easily covering more ground.

He reached the treasure at the same time as the Sandpipers' captain, shifting back to human form with his hand outstretched. But the two rivals snatched it at the same time.

It was a tie.

The spectators watching from the stands went wild trying to see if the Cardinals took the win. They had watched the whole thing: the struggle over the rocks, how they'd washed down the river, all of it.

"The Cardinals are the strongest Louper team with four consecutive wins," said Izzie to anyone who would listen. Alison smiled at her best friend.

But before the spell ended, Luke and the captain held up their hands together with the gold disc between them.

"It's a draw," gasped Aya.

The spell ended, and the other team disappeared, back on their school grounds, and all that remained on the field were the worn and weary Cardinals.

"We'll see them in the finals." David declared.

"That should be fun," Luke muttered.

The fans filled the field and ran to the Cardinals, treating them like heroes and raising Luke and David up on their shoulders. Luke reached down to grasp Izzie's hand for a moment before the crowd carried him away, still cheering

CHAPTER FIFTEEN

April Fool's Day was just around the corner, and this year everyone assumed Ethan would lay it aside. Enough tension was in the air from the missing student that no one was in the mood for it.

Every year, Ethan had found a prank to pull on the school. It was something of a tradition—it broke the tension when everyone was working hard to pass their classes, and it was all in the name of fun.

But they underestimated Ethan. He started looking around to see what he could do. He wanted something fun, something lighthearted, something different. And this time, he wanted to do something better than before. This time, he wanted to go all out.

"I don't suppose you can be talked out of it. What are you going to do?" Peter and Ethan were sitting under the tall old trees by the tennis courts. Dorvu was perched just overhead, snorting snowflakes.

"I don't know. I want to do something that really wows

everyone. Something crazier than before. Everyone could use something else to think about."

"I don't think that's what anyone had in mind. You know, if you get caught doing something crazier than before, your punishment is going to be crazier than before."

Ethan nodded. He had been punished every time he pulled a prank—cleaning up after Dorvu was the worst. But when a prank worked well, then the consequences were so worth it.

"I don't want to pull anyone else into this. Although, a little help would be great. But I'm not going to let anyone else take the fall if it goes wrong."

"How noble of you." Peter chuckled.

Ethan caught himself before he nudged Peter—he didn't want to hurt his friend who was still recovering from the beating he took. Instead, he shrugged, gently nudging his friend.

"I'll figure something out," he said. "Something eye-popping!"

Ethan brainstormed for days. The professors had unwittingly loaded his arsenal with their lesson plans. He knew he could pull out all the stops and really make it count. The further he continued with his schooling, the better his pranks were getting. He could only imagine what he would be able to do during his senior year.

Finally, Ethan settled on a prank.

Over the next couple of days, he snuck off the grounds

whenever he could. He knew it was dangerous—look at what had happened to Peter. But he wasn't going to a bar to spy on some dark wizards because he wanted to find answers. He was headed out to create a prank that would be remembered for years after he left the School of Necessary Magic.

That's the way you create a legacy.

The more Ethan thought about it, the more he liked it. He could be a legend—one of the students that future students would talk about endlessly, and one they would try to copy.

Finally, the first day of April arrived. And it was perfect conditions—he had been watching the forecast for days, hoping for weather just like this.

Early that morning, students filed into the dining hall for breakfast. Ethan was in the front of the group, glancing out one of the tall windows.

"What's so interesting out there?"

A pixie fluttered through the air in front of him, startling him.

"Huh? Nothing, just checking the weather."

"Really?" The pixie tilted her head to the side and lifted a large ladle, shaking it in front of Ethan's face. "We have our eye on you, kiddo. We all know what day it is. Still haven't gotten over the time you changed the sugar into salt. Not funny, except for maybe Mary Anne and that big spoonful…"

The pixie flitted away but turned back. "Just keep your paws off the kitchen. I know it's too much to ask a hormonal wizard to mind his own business completely."

She flew closer to his face again, almost making him see

cross-eyed. "If you don't, just remember, payback is a bitch in the form of a pixie."

He could feel the tiny bit of spray as she spat the last words and flew back to the confines of the kitchen.

"Good to know," he muttered, looking back outside. The clouds were gray, creating a thick blanket over the countryside and promising the type of weather that made everyone want to sip a cup of hot chocolate. The humidity had been rising slowly over the past couple of days, and a thunderstorm was finally here.

Thunder rumbled through the air, and lightning cracked just outside the windows. Inside, his friends were already seated at their table, plowing through breakfast.

"Why are you so quiet, Ethan?" Luke skewered a mouthful of pancakes, stuffing it into his mouth.

Ethan shrugged as raindrops began to hit the window panes. He sat down and let his wand slide out of his sleeve.

"Perfect. *Apertus Portalus.*" Ethan whispered under his breath, clutching his wand beneath the table. Immediately, a large portal opened in the dining hall ceiling, and rain started pouring through. Frogs emerged out of the corners of the wall, hopping between the students' feet, sending up screams and squeals of laughter. Snakes slithered down the walls, hissing as they got to the floor.

The students jumped up, yelling, and ran to the walls where the rain couldn't reach. Thunder rumbled again, and lightning snapped right against the ceiling where dark clouds had created the sky inside the school building. Despite trying to hide from the rain, many of the students were dripping wet in mere seconds.

188

"Was this you?" Peter pointed at Ethan, standing by the side, laughing. He just smiled.

He looked at the chaos and held up his wand, out in the open this time, and said in a clear voice, "*Restoras Springtime. Portalus Perdus.*" The portal closed, and the water drained out of the large hall, seeping out of the hair and clothing and disappearing from the plates and tops of tables. The frogs let out their last loud chorus of croaks and transformed into vines of flowers, curling around the table legs. The snakes became butterflies floating up to the ceiling, bursting into different colored lights.

Sunlight shone in through the windows, even as the storm continued around the rest of the building.

"Well done, Master Ethan," said Professor Powell, a look of admiration mixed with his perpetual scowl.

"Brilliant, right?" Ethan raised his arms in a large 'V', waiting for the applause.

"You're going to be in a hell of a lot of trouble." Luke checked his backpack again. The frogs who had taken refuge in it were gone, replaced by flowers.

Ethan shrugged. "Maybe. I think I have a fifty-fifty chance."

"Ethan!" Mara beckoned to him. "Let's talk."

"I guess I'm in trouble." Ethan marched off with her to the hallway.

"What do you think you're doing?" she asked. Her arms crossed, and an eyebrow arched.

"Can't tell if I'm going to be cleaning toilets with a toothbrush or not."

"It's an interesting thought." She tapped her fingers on

her elbows. "First, congratulations on pulling off that spell. Not an easy one."

Ethan smiled smugly then froze when he saw the look in the headmistress' eyes.

"Secondly," she added, "I get what you were trying to do. This has been a pretty dismal place this semester. I can't say I've been able to figure out a way to help. You just did that. Thank you."

"What?" Ethan looked like he was going to fall over with surprise.

"Don't let it go to your head. You figured out a way to use magic to help everyone. That's always a good thing, even if this was a little... odd. But, magic is tricky. You may not always be so lucky. Just remember, consequences go with every action."

"But you liked it... I'm not in trouble?"

"I take it very little of what I'm saying is sinking in." Mara let out a deep sigh. "Very well, yes, you're not in trouble. Happy April Fool's Day. You're the rightful leader of this day. Irony abounds."

The bell rang overhead.

"Get to class and don't pull anything else today. I can always change my mind."

But he was already gone, taking the stairs two at a time, a wide smile across his face.

"Better hope those pixies feel the same way. They have memories that go on for days."

CHAPTER SIXTEEN

In the boys' freshman dorm, a young wizard named Frank was up at the crack of dawn, greeting the day. Today was Professor Fowler's class on the use of mushrooms to ward off diseases in magicals. He hoped to be a doctor for magicals someday and had looked forward to this class all week.

The rest of his roommates were still asleep. Norman, his best friend, put his pillow over his face, mumbling something about, "go back to sleep!" before rolling over.

Frank pulled on his shoes and ignored the different grumbles as he tied them. The morning was beautiful. It had rained the past few days, but it was clear now. It was going to be a great day.

When he first came to the school, he was worried about being away from his parents for so long. But freshman year wasn't nearly as bad as he thought it would be, and on Halloween, he even got to speak to his dead great-grandfather, another Frank, and tell him all about homecoming. Every day he felt more like he belonged.

Once Frank was dressed, he left the room, and went down the wide stairs, poking his head into the common room, looking around for the squirrel.

"No sign of him," he whispered, stepping out further. "This really is a good day." He pulled out his phone and made his daily check-in call. "Hi Mom, it's me. Yes, I'm okay. No, I haven't seen anything strange. I'm good." It was the deal he made with his parents after time had passed, and the missing student still wasn't found. Not even a clue.

"I have to get to breakfast. Yes, I'll check in again tomorrow. Nice to hear your voice, too." He hung up, sliding the phone into his pocket. "Geez, worriers."

Frank walked down the stairs and out the front door, heading toward the barns. He had lied, as usual. The dining hall wasn't open yet. But he liked being able to look out over the woods and say hello to the dragon before heading back around the grounds. His late great-grandfather had called it a constitutional.

The sun rose above the horizon, coloring the world again, and there were only a few puffs of clouds in the sky. Frank rounded the main building, touching the large granite cornerstone, slowing down. A loud buzzing was drawing his attention.

"What are bees…" He looked around for Horace in his beekeeper's uniform, but no one else was in sight.

He came completely around the corner and saw the source of the buzzing. "It is bees."

A giant swarm of bees was gathered over the grass in the center of the courtyard. There were so many of them that they looked like a dark cloud, churning and buzzing, and changing shape.

"Hey! Hey!" Frank looked back to see if there was anyone else to come and help him. In the center of the swarm, Frank could just make out something hovering in mid-air, something long, and dark and oblong.

He squinted his eyes, putting his hand up to shade the morning sun.

"Can't tell exactly…" Words failed him. He nervously tapped the phone in his pocket. "Maybe I should call…" But even as he said it, he walked closer to the grassy area.

As he came closer, the shape in the middle started to lower, as if it wanted Frank to come closer to inspect it.

Suddenly, he froze. His mouth gaped open. He stared at what the bees had exposed.

It was the missing student. She had been stung by so many bees that her body was bloated and swollen with red patches covering her. Her eyes were closed—swollen shut —her hair hung down in strings as she hovered just above the ground, the bees humming and buzzing around her as if this was their queen. Or they were holding her up. Or something.

Frank fell to his knees and threw up. He squeezed his eyes shut, the buzzing suddenly grating against his very bones as he began to scream, squeezing his fists at his side.

The doors behind him crashed open as Professor Grant ran to see what was wrong.

"What's happened?" Her hair was loose around her shoulders "Oh… dear… God…"

Frank rocked on the ground, his eyes still shut although he wasn't screaming anymore.

"Frank, come with me." The professor was gently whispering, not taking her eyes off the limp body hanging in the front of the school. She pulled out her wand and twirled it in a circle over her head. "Experiallus!" The blue line of magic twirled out of her wand, splitting into different directions to alert the staff.

The blue light buzzed at Professor Cooper's shoulder until he rolled over, the four pupils focusing on the light. "Come quick and bring help. Lisa has been found in the front courtyard." Professor Grant's message was short and full of alarm. He jumped up, pulling on jeans, not bothering with shoes. All over the grounds, professors came running from their cottages, slamming doors and shouting out questions.

He ran up to find Annabelle Grant trying to convince Frank Morgan, the young wizard to get up.

"Come inside," she said gently.

"She's dead," Frank said in a soft voice.

Grant nodded, "Yes, I believe she is."

Tears rolled down Frank's cheek, and he was angry that he was crying. But he stood and let Grant guide him into the building as more professors converged in the courtyard, stopping short of the bees still hovering over the body.

Mara came out, already forming a fireball in her hands. She leaned back like a pitcher and hurled the flames at the swarm, scattering them.

They returned, regrouping around the edges. Professor Hodges let out a low growl, scattering them again. He moved in closer. The bees shifted into a straight line and flew away.

"If I didn't know better, I'd say those bees just followed an order." Professor Hudson watched them go, flying through the fields.

The headmistress reached out and pulled Lisa toward her, cradling the body gently against her. She didn't care that the girl was dead—might have been dead for a while, or that her body was beyond recognition from all the poison in her system. She was treating her as though Lisa still needed to be consoled and could feel the warm, gentle embrace.

Students crowded at the windows, staring out and pointing, and pulling out their phones, talking. Mara nodded to Professor Hudson, who raised her wand, drawing a veil of darkness between Mara and anyone else.

"Thank you," whispered Mara.

"It's the least we can do."

On the way up the front steps, Mara passed Jason Parker.

Jason looked at the body with curiosity and disgust. As the headmistress passed him, the girl's face slipped to the side as if she was looking at Jason. Her eyes were swollen shut, but there was no doubt who this was.

It was Lisa.

Jason pressed his fist into his stomach, stumbling backward. "I never," he said it too quietly for anyone to hear.

Mara took Lisa's body to the infirmary. There was nothing that could be done for her, but it was the safest place to take her. One by one, the professors joined her. Xander Powell still keeping his distance.

Professor Hodges helped lay Lisa's body out on a bed. The professors were all around her. Tears welled up in their eyes, and mouths pressed into thin lines.

"This was staged for our benefit." Mara moved a stray piece of hair out of the girl's bloated face. "Whoever did this wanted one of us to find the body."

"It wasn't just a scare tactic. It was a warning." Xander Powell practically shouted the words.

The school nurse came and shooed them all away. "Enough. Let me look after the dear girl."

"Take care of her." Mara hurried out of the infirmary ignoring Professor Powell calling her name.

"What do you want?" Leo Decker stood in the door of the library like he was standing guard. "Ma'am," he added respectfully, even though he sounded grumpier than ever. The poppy on his bowler hat hissed and spat at Mara, baring its teeth. She hissed back, surprising it and causing the flower to close its petals.

"I need very specific information about old, dark magic. A forbidden spell from the last time Oriceran was connected to Earth."

Leo shrugged, rubbing his chin. "What exactly, specifically? There's a lot of darkness from that era."

"From the days the magicals could control the insects and animals. Anything that flew or walked or slithered on the ground."

"That is ancient. I have something on that, but we're forbidden even to open it. Only the Gardener of the Dark

Forest remembers any of those spells. Maybe his son, Perrom."

"Open it!" she snapped. "Do it anyway. I need to look at what's in the vault."

Leo narrowed his eyes at her. "No one goes into the vault. No one has even seen the inside aside from the gnomes, and we rarely go inside."

"It's important, Leo. A student is dead, and I think that spell was the weapon. I need to find answers."

"Blast the two moons and a thousand trolls," Leo grumbled something else that was inaudible arguing with himself. Finally, he nodded and turned around. "I can see your point. Have to protect our own," he muttered, making his way to the back of the library.

Mara did not need an invitation to follow him. They walked through the library, shelves towering on each side of them holding the history or instructions for most of the light magic. The farther back they went, the more the shelves became spaced out, and stacks of books were piled up on the floor between them. Ancient tomes considered safe to read but only by well-trained magicals. There was a host of answers to be found between those pages.

"Not what you're looking for." Leo hurried past them. "No point in wasting your time."

Finally, at the very back of the library, Leo pushed open the fenced cage door leading into the restricted section. At the back stood the vault's heavy door. "Stand aside." He waved at the gnomes standing guard. They reluctantly moved out of the way, looking back and forth at each other.

Leo gestured for Mara to step in first and closed the door behind her. "In case anything goes wrong."

"Goes wrong?"

"Just opening the book is trouble."

Mara heard the locking mechanism shut them in and shivered. The librarian snapped his fingers, turning on the lights inside the vault.

Mara gazed around in awe, despite the dark occasion. She was standing among books that were so riddled with magic, they had become artifacts.

Leo put on gloves, carefully lifting different tomes and setting them aside. "A cousin of mine made these for me. Helps stop any of the old magic from getting on my skin. Can cause a terrible rash and itch for days. Ah, here we are."

He lifted a large book with gold edging and laid it on top of the pile. "You sure about this? Some things, once you get them started, you can't go back."

"I'm sure. There's been enough harm caused already. Too much. We have to risk it."

"Suit yourself. Warning delivered. From here, you go it alone." The gnome clapped his hands, disappearing in a blue puff of smoke.

Mara rolled her eyes. "I forgot about that. Sneaky little shit. Fine, I'll go it alone. May the luck of Yumfuck be with me." She took a deep breath, letting it out slowly as she raised the edge of the cover.

Tiny moths flew up and circled her head in a halo. She kept her breathing even and turned the first page as the lettering appeared. Set an intention was written on the page.

"Find me a killer," she whispered, wondering what she was setting free. "Tell me who dared to control the bees."

Alison and Izzie sat together in their room. Izzie stared at her shoes, kicking at something invisible on the floor. Alison's face was turned to the window, but she didn't see anything. Her mind was wandering—it had come as a terrible shock to find out that Lisa had died. They could still sense what each other was feeling.

"I really thought we'd find her."

"Me too. We all did," her voice trailed off.

"She's dead. I can't believe it. How could this happen?"

"Bee stings, a lot of them."

Alison shook her head. "I'm not talking about how she died. I'm talking about how someone got into the school. They *still* haven't figured that out."

"Do you still think Xander Powell had anything to do with this? I can't believe he's that twisted. That takes a special kind of dark."

"It's hard to believe anyone out there would do something like that. I don't know." She turned away from the window. "I think he knows more than he's saying. We need to find out what that is."

"Does that scare you?" Izzie asked. "It feels so random. Who could be next?"

"No, it doesn't," Alison said. "It makes me think that it's someone on the inside."

"You really will make a good bounty hunter. I know you mean Jason Parker."

Since the connection spell, every theory Alison had about Jason flowed between the three of them on the silver thread that tied them together. Izzie knew exactly what Alison suspected, and that she had nothing to prove it.

"The very same. I can just feel it. But we need to find proof. We need to find something that points us in the right direction."

"How do you want to do that?" Izzie asked.

"I think we need to go to the freshman boys," Alison said.

"Why?" Izzie said. "I don't think Frank will know anything, even though he was the one to discover the body. Can you imagine? He's going to be scarred for life."

"We all are in some way or another," Alison said, pounding her fist into the bed. "But no, that's not why I want to speak to the freshmen. I saw Jason speaking to another freshman just after we came back from Christmas break. The kid looked like he was buying some long story, and when Jason saw us, he put on a smile—a forced one."

Alison and Izzie left the dorms on a mission. They searched the campus and quickly found a group of freshmen, Frank among them, sitting in the corner of the library. He was doing his best to look like he was reading, but his hand was trembling where it held the page.

The teenager Alison saw with Jason was sitting in the middle.

Alison glanced at Izzie, and they nodded at each other.

"We want answers, and we want them now," Izzie said in a stern voice. The teenagers looked at her and frowned.

"Anything you've learned," Alison said, forming balls of

light in her hands. "What do you know about what's been going on around campus?"

They all shook their heads, and a few of them snickered.

"Why should we tell you anything? We don't owe you anything."

"Yeah, go play somewhere else."

Frank looked up nervously, sliding his chair away from the group.

"Freaks."

"Can't even control your magic."

Izzie's forehead wrinkled. "Gonna make it personal. Works for me." Her eyes glowed, and the symbols lit up across her arms. Streaks of light flowed from her fingers and swirled around the boys. Not hot enough to burn them, but enough to make an impression. It wouldn't leave a mark, but it got the message across.

Frank ducked under the table, pulling his backpack in with him.

"It was just for fun. We're sorry."

"That's fun? Who's the real freak?"

"What do you mean? What are you talking about?"

"We thought it would be cool to prank the guys the same way Ethan did. We'll stop. We promise."

Izzie shook her head. "Try again."

"That's not what we're talking about," Alison said, struggling to keep a stern voice. "What else do you know? What have you done?"

"I skipped Professor Powell's class and went down to the kemana instead to hang out with a willen. He's teaching me how to pick pockets."

"I put a spell over the toilet in Professor Powell's bathroom. It flushed up for an entire day."

"I called my mom and asked her to fetch me, told her I was scared, but I just wanted to miss Hodges' quiz."

"I set the mouse plants free in Professor Fowler's room. I had no idea they'd reproduce all night."

"I glued down the pots in the kitchen, but it was only a temporary spell. Fifteen minutes tops! Please don't tell the pixies. They can hold a grudge."

They were all talking over each other, terrified of Izzie's magic and staring at the symbols passing along her arms.

Every transgression they had ever committed in their lives came spilling out.

"Enough!" Alison shook her head.

"Clearly, not criminal masterminds." Izzie's eyes stopped glowing. "Except for maybe you, willen boy." The boys looked relieved, just one looking away under Izzie's gaze.

"I'm not talking about every single thing you've ever done wrong." Alison put her hands on her hips. "Let's try this again. I'm talking about what happened this morning. Did you guys notice anything different? Did anyone say anything that seemed suspicious?"

Alison kept an eye on the freshman who was seen talking to Jason. He kept staring at a scratch in the library table. Alison used her senses instead of her glasses to look at him and see his soul energy. But she didn't see guilt or remorse. All she saw was green shades of nervousness. "He doesn't know anything."

"Dead end again."

"Well, I did notice something." Frank poked his head out from under the table.

"What?" Izzie pulled out his chair, waiting for him to sit.

"The bees. They've been everywhere. I like to think of myself as an apiarist."

"A what?"

"He means a beekeeper." A tall, skinny teen with stringy brown hair piped up. "He likes to use big fancy words when five small ones would do just as well."

"Ignore them, just look at me." Izzie sent out energy to combine with Frank's, calming him.

"They arrived too early this year. It was strange for the season. They seem to have had a mind of their own."

Alison nodded. "Thank you, boys." She nudged Izzie, and the two of them left the library.

Izzie came to a halt outside of the library. "What did you find out?" Izzie asked. "All I heard was something we already knew."

Alison shook her head. "The kid is right. The bees are a good clue. Think about it—they were here much earlier than usual. And they were usually just one or two, but bees are usually part of a hive."

"Until they swarmed over that girl." Izzie's whole body shuddered.

"It doesn't make sense unless you add magic."

"If that's the case, we're talking dark magic. The darkest. You're pretty good at this, Alison. Your dad would be proud."

"Maybe it really is my calling to become a bounty hunter someday."

CHAPTER SEVENTEEN

Classes didn't resume until the next day. Everyone needed a distraction. Alison and Izzie and their group sat in Multi-dimensional class staring up at Professor Wilson.

"I know it's not easy to deal with what happened, but I have an idea." He looked over at the box of multi-dimensional glasses and stood up, grabbing it.

"After something terrible like this happens, the worst thing is to do nothing at all. It's not good to mull over the events. That's how nightmares are created."

He handed out the glasses to the first row of students. "Put them on," he said when they looked at him, confused. "I only have the five pairs right now, but this will work. We'll take turns."

When the first row of students' glasses was in place, the professor cast a spell. As he mumbled the words, small sparks danced between the students' glasses, heads, and chests as the magic took effect.

As soon as the spell was cast, each student found themselves in their favorite place in the world. The magic took it from their memories.

"I want each of you to be able to escape, just for an hour, and remember what it's like to feel protected. That still exists, even here."

Peter closed his eyes and watched the images flashing in front of him. He stood in the middle of a green field on his grandfather's ranch. His favorite place to go during the summer vacations. The mountains in the distance were tall, purple shadows with snow-capped tips, and the sky was a clear blue. The air had a bite to it as it often did, and he whistled long and low. His gray mare came to him at a trot. She squealed, happy to see him. He reached out to her velvet nose and stroked it as she nuzzled his pockets, looking for a snack. He felt his shoulders relax and he let out a contented sigh.

Ethan was in his childhood room back home, pictures of his favorite kid's movies against the walls, and Bingo, his old Labrador that had passed away, lay at the foot of his bed, wagging his tail, happy to see him. He ran to the dog.

"B-I-N-G-O, B-I-N-G-O, B-I-N-G-O, and Bingo was his name-o," he sang to his dog as he always had. The rest of the class laughed, and the tension slowly broke as the students found their happy places and let go of the pain and tension.

Alison watched as the students relaxed. Professor Wilson's idea was working. She watched their energy slowly go from dark blue of sorrow to a vibrant green or light pink.

"It's working."

When it was finally her turn, Alison put the glasses on. She hoped she would finally be able to see her mother again. She missed her very much. When the glasses were finally in place, Alison didn't see the woman who had raised her and been ripped away from her far too soon. Instead, she only saw a swirl of the loving energy she had known as her mother.

A pang of disappointment shot into her chest. "I should have known this would happen. I never saw her." She did her best to hide her disappointment, handing the glasses to Izzie, who was up next.

Izzie took the glasses from Alison and took a deep breath before putting them on. "Okay, I'll admit it, I'm nervous."

"It'll be okay. I'm right here."

"Here we go. Happy pictures from the orphanage. Sure, why not?"

Izzie slipped the glasses onto her face and felt the magic spark between her heart, her mind, and the glasses. The magic created an image before her, but it had nothing to do with the orphanage where she remembered growing up.

Instead, she was sitting on a white framed bed in a pink room that felt familiar. A man with long, straight blonde hair sat on the edge of her bed and was singing. "Be a little bird…" he sang. A woman with dark hair was sitting next to her, with her arms wrapped around Izzie's shoulders. It was still too difficult to make out her face.

She felt wrapped in so much love and affection, and when she looked at the man who was singing, his face was almost visible. "Dad." The words slipped out of her before she could think about it. She looked at the blurry image of the woman. "Mom, it's you. It's a real memory. I'm sure of it." She was practically shouting as she reached out to try and touch the images.

Tears rolled down her cheeks before she could stop them. She reached forward again, trying to touch her dad, but instead, her hands only swiped through thin air.

The spell faded, and so did the memory. "Wait! What are your names? My name! What is my name?" She reluctantly removed the glasses and handed them off, the feelings lingering. "I saw them again. I know they're real!" She gripped Alison's arm, excited. "Do you know what that means? Maybe we can find them."

"Are you sure it wasn't what you wanted to see?" asked Kathleen.

"No, it was a real memory," said Alison. "I could feel it too."

"So could I." Tanner sat there, ashen.

"You guys want to explain something?" asked Professor Wilson.

"Extracurricular activity. We were practicing a spell and…"

"Do I want to know this? Was anyone hurt? Did you break anything?"

"No to all three." Tanner gave him a wink.

The bell rang, saving them from having to explain any further.

Izzie rubbed her face, getting rid of the tears. "My parents are real. I'm not alone after all."

"You never were," whispered Alison.

"Now what?" asked Aya.

"I got this one," said Jennifer. "We find them, of course."

"Sounds about right," said Alison.

"Dodge ball!" Kathleen pumped her fist in the air. "Let's do this!" They were gathered in the gym, dressed in their gym uniforms of a white shirt and maroon shorts.

"It's not the Louper tournament." Emma pulled her blonde hair back into a scrunchie. "Chill. Remember? A girl is still dead. They're making us stick to our schedule because the grown-ups think it will help us."

"Like we won't remember that a swarm of bees killed somebody on school grounds."

"We don't know that it was on the grounds."

"That doesn't help."

"Kathleen's right. Let's see if we can let it go for one match." Alison found a spot along the outer left side. The best position to evade the ball in the first crucial moments.

"Of course, you'd say that." Izzie stretched an arm over her head. "You always win."

"There should be something in the rules about watching the energy of a magic ball." Aya stood near Alison, with her hands out, ready to dive on the ground.

"Better dive quick, Aya. That ball can change directions like that!" Izzie snapped her fingers.

Professor Grant held the magic red rubber ball the size of a large pumpkin up over her head. It was vibrating in her hand, waiting for the command that would release it. "Everyone ready? No? Well, girls, better *get* ready." She smiled, her long brown hair framing her face. "Here we go!" She blew the whistle, letting go of the rubber ball

The ball hovered for a moment, whizzing out in a zigzag line picking off the slower girls.

Whomp! Whomp!

Two girls fell to the ground, the red rubber stinging against their skin.

"Ooooh, the ball came to play. Taking them out early." Izzie ran as fast as she could, pulling in energy and using it to sense the ball behind her, then dove for the floor at the last moment. The ball sailed right over her head, barely missing her, and took out a sophomore with short brown hair.

"Ooof!" The girl caught the ball in the midsection, landing backward. The wind knocked out of her momentarily.

"Good effort, Lainie! Only two seconds. Three seconds more, and you would have won. I admire your effort!" Professor Grant blew the whistle as the ball circled the outside then zinged into the center and smacked Aya in the head, taking her out.

Alison watched as the ball changed direction and headed straight at Izzie. "Duck!" she shouted. Izzie stepped out of the way at the last possible second. Kathleen was right behind her and grabbed on to the ball.

The ball went wild, jerking Kathleen around, lifting her off her feet and dangling her in the air. "Wooooohoooo! Wheeeee!" Kathleen held on for dear life, and after five seconds—which felt like an eternity—she won the game.

Alison could see how happy she was, the colors in her soul brightening, the colors rolling through her energy.

Izzie smiled, too. "You did it!"

Kathleen was grinning from ear to ear, her hair coming

out of her ponytail. She looked wild and reckless, and the look suited her.

"I'm glad we had this, even for a little while." Izzie rested her hands on her knees, breathing a little hard. The memory of the man and woman was still playing in her mind. *My real parents are out there. I know that now.*

"I know what you're thinking." Alison stood in front of her best friend. "I can feel it, you know. You have a family here, too. No matter what happens, we all stick together."

"Together." Kathleen and Aya nodded. Jennifer put her arm around Emma's neck. "Go Cardinals, for life! I am pumped!"

CHAPTER EIGHTEEN

Professor Lucy Fowler was waiting for them in her classroom. Her wild, red hair was tied back with a silver bandanna. She wore a busy floral smock over dark blue overalls. Her reputation around the school was an eccentric teacher who thought outside the box, just the way she liked it. She was also one of the most powerful Light Elves in the country, and everyone respected her skill using flora in magic.

"You guys look spent," she said, as everyone sat down.

"I feel pretty good." Kathleen slid into her seat.

Izzie smiled at her, lingering at the window. The view was of the circular driveway. Her friends joined her at the window, growing quiet.

Professor Fowler thought for a moment before she nodded. "Yeah, yeah, I think we need to do something fun today."

"What are we going to do?" Emma pulled herself away from the window.

"We are going to plant Lavender Corbal." Fowler picked up one of the lacy purple plants in a red clay pot and stroked the leaves. The plant responded, cooing and emitting a soothing scent. "Oriceran's version of laughing gas. A little temporary relief." She held up a finger. "Approved for use, not to worry. Okay, gather up your gardening tools, let's head outside."

Professor Fowler understood that the students were too nervous to go anywhere near the front of the building where Lisa's body was found, and the entire area was still cordoned off with a ring of magic.

"This way girls. This way." She led them around the back of the building, along a curving brick path to the gardens in the back, and into the courtyard where Sophie was found. Alison saw her chance and chose the gardening bed near the spot, hoping to find a clue.

"I know what you're up to." Izzie knelt next to her. "I can feel what you're feeling."

"I didn't forget. Help me look."

Tanner dropped down next to them. "Count me in. Maybe there's something."

Professor Fowler passed out the Lavender Corbal plants wrapped in small, burlap bags.

The dragon let out a long, mournful cry overhead, swooping over the school.

Alison looked up, and a smile spread across her face. "Of course, Dorvu. No one has asked him what he saw."

"I get it. The bird's eye view."

Izzie dug the tip of her spade in the dirt and felt it hit against something solid. "We may not need to." She kept digging around, uncovering a metal box.

"It's an artifact."

"Don't touch that!" Professor Fowler stood over their shoulders staring down at the box. "It's a marker," she gasped. "Works like an energy absorbent and weakens protective spells. I think we may have discovered how they're getting in. Good job teen magicals!"

"Now, we need to figure out how they got out."

"Oh, we're not done, ladies. One of these wouldn't do it. It would take at least a few dozen of them, and they're dangerous. That little thing has got to be filled with the energy from every glamour we've put on this school. It could go off like a bomb!" Professor Fowler opened her hand, rolling a ball of light and gently pitching it into the air. It split into dozens of smaller balls that raced across the grounds.

"What is that going to do?" Izzie watched one of them brighten and hover just outside the courtyard.

"Found another! Well done! They can sense the excess energy and tag it. Only dozens more to go."

Mara walked through the first-floor hallway of the old manor. She listened to the sounds of footsteps as the last child ran into a classroom just as Professor Powell yelled that the door was closing.

Mara winced at the sound of his deep baritone. She walked past the old portraits. *Nothing has been able to stop the darkness from getting in here. Not the magic around the school that should have been impenetrable, not the extra guards around the school. Nothing.*

Mara stopped at the front door and leaned against the door frame. Her old friend, Professor Hudson came up next to her.

"You know, there was a time when I believed these doors could keep anyone out."

"Was that last week?" Eleanor Hudson looked out over the green lawn, past the magical barriers hovering around the driveway.

"Something like that."

"What now?"

"We keep going. If we stop, they win by default. I can't have that."

"That's all I needed to hear. I'll stand by your side for as long as the school stays open."

"That's all I needed to hear."

"You already knew." Eleanor gave her old friend a hug. They turned and walked down the West Wing hallway to where the classes were located.

The classroom doors were located on both sides of the corridor with a large glass pane in the top of each door. The headmistress stopped at each class, looking in from the hallway.

"It's a little quiet but otherwise normal. A miracle really." Professor Hudson watched Professor Grant working with her students.

"I have a confession." Mara walked down the hall a little farther with Professor Hudson right behind her. "Since Lisa disappeared, I haven't been able to shake the feeling that something else is going to go wrong any moment."

"I think they call that sanity."

"No, this feels more like an actual warning." She put her hand on her belly. "Even if it's only a false alarm, I have to pay attention to it. Something bad is coming."

"How bad?"

"The last stand, maybe. They're coming to try and take down the school. I'm telling you; I can feel it."

"Then let's prepare for the battle."

"I don't know if I can handle another incident. One student dead, one suffering from a traumatic magical attack, and two students in the infirmary. Four cases that should never have happened."

"Dark times. Let's prepare. It will give everyone something to do and a common mission. We've been flailing around here, trying to act like everything is normal. Maybe it's time we gave up on that and act like we're at war because we are."

"Good speech. You've been waiting to tell me that for a while, haven't you?"

"Also, since last week."

"It's been a busy week. I'm going to check in on the classrooms. Keep me in the loop while you're building up of our forces."

"Of course, fearless leader."

Mara smiled, watching her friend smile as she walked away. She walked slowly down the hallway, looking briefly into each classroom.

"Bzzzzzzzzz. Bzzzzzzz. Bzzzzzzz." The magical buzz from the front door let her know someone was there to see her. The moment she had been dreading was here. Lisa's parents had arrived to get the entire story.

She turned on her heel and walked back to her office to welcome her guests the best she could.

When Mara arrived at her office, she found the parents huddled on her small couch, sitting stone-faced. Mara came in and softly shut the door behind her. *Eleanor is right. We need to prepare for the battle that's coming.*

CHAPTER NINETEEN

Izzie and Alison waited until the other roommates were asleep before they slipped out of bed and shrugged into coats. It wasn't nearly as cold as it was just a month before, but the evening breeze still had a bite to it and wandering around in pajamas would have them freezing half to death.

Once they were bundled up, Izzie and Alison quietly snuck out of the dorm, taking care to make as little sound as possible. There was a strict curfew in place, and it was going to take a little magic to get them out the door, undetected.

Izzie followed behind Alison, muttering words beneath her breath. She was bending the light, just as she'd learned in school, to hide them from detection.

Finally, when they were outside, the girls let out a breath. They had made it without being spotted by any of the guards that Mara had stationed on the grounds.

Izzie looked up at the sky. It was a moonless night, and darkness covered the spaces between the lamp posts. It made it hard to navigate past the main buildings while making it easier to cross the fields to get closer to the woods.

There was a gentle flapping of wings above them, and Alison stepped back as Dorvu landed at their feet, now standing well above their heads.

"You should be inside." The dragon still sounded like a teenage girl, even if it was a deep baritone. It was a leftover from his days in their care inside the egg. "Too dangerous out here."

"Actually, we needed to speak to you."

The dragon let out a sigh, ice crystals blowing out of his nostrils. He smacked his lips together, gnashing his large, sharp teeth. "I am always here for you."

He spread his large silver wings, shook them out, blowing the girls hair back and making their eyes water.

Alison pushed her glasses up firmly on her nose. "You know about the dead girl, Lisa May, right?"

"I saw what happened with the bees."

"You watch over us on a pretty regular basis, don't you?" Izzie stroked the long, scaly nose, unafraid of Dorvu.

"You're my family. I'm always here for you."

Izzie stretched her arms across the great neck, hugging the dragon. "Have you seen anyone suspicious wandering on the grounds?"

"This place is full of teenagers. I see suspicious things on the hour."

"Anything that struck you as different?"

"Now, that's a different story. There have been those who slip around the back of the dining hall, waiting until the pixies are distracted. It looked like they were planting something."

"The energy blockers! Why didn't you say anything?"

"No one was asking."

"Can you describe them?"

"Puny magical. You all kind of look alike to me."

"Young puny magical or older?"

"Definitely older."

"When's the last time you saw them?"

"The middle of last night. They were headed to the old storm cellar."

"There's a storm cellar?"

"Show us," said Alison. "Fly above us, and we'll track you."

"For you, anything. Love the new glasses. I'm obsessed." The dragon pushed off, the wind pushing down around them.

"It's weird when he talks just like us, right?"

"Totally."

Alison pushed her glasses onto the top of her head and focused on the energy that she could see all around her. Her glasses didn't help her at all if she was shrouded in darkness. The moment she pushed the glasses onto her head, the world around her came to life. She grabbed Izzie's hand to guide her, following the magic that pulsed in the area and seeing everything by the power it gave off rather than the images.

Above them, the dragon screeched a mournful cry. They tracked him down behind the main buildings and halfway to the barns to the hidden storm cellar. The only thing visible was the thick, wooden door flush with the ground.

"I've never noticed this part of the grounds before."

"I didn't realize this was even usable back here." Stands of old growth trees tangled with twisting vines and dense weeds.

"This may be what the dark families were using to hide."

Izzie held her hands close together, and between her palms, a ball of light sprung into existence and grew until it was the size of a tennis ball. She balanced the light so that it hovered just above her fingertips, using it as a torch, as Alison used her Drow energy to wrench the cellar door open.

Alison slipped her glasses back onto her nose. She still had the colors of magic in her peripheral vision, but for the moment she relied on her magical eyesight.

They crept down the stone steps that smelled of mildew and peered into the dimly lit room. Cobwebs hung from the rafters and clung to an old bench. "It doesn't look like anyone has been here. This is a dead end."

Izzie was already halfway up the stairs, holding up the ball of light.

"Oh, okay, already moving out." Alison took a last glance around, but the wide-open room was empty. "I was so sure," she muttered, heading up the stairs to catch up with Izzie.

Dorvu disturbed a flock of birds sleeping in a tall pine tree, and they took flight, shaking the branches. The dragon circled overhead, a large shadow against the dark night, letting out a rumbling roar.

Alison and Izzie finally reached the barn. A light shone through the wide-open doors. Horace was in his usual spot. Standing next to him was his Aunt Estelle. They both had the same flaming red hair and noses straight as an arrow.

Horace was thumbing through a book and closed it when he saw the girls.

Estelle took a deep drag on her cigarette and blew a cloud of smoke that floated just above her bouffant. "Taking a stroll? You seem to make a habit of being out on the grounds when the world has gone quiet."

"Things seem to make more sense this time of night." Izzie reached out to pet Horace's dog as he stood up and shook his large head.

"I do know you." Izzie let the magic reach out, circling Estelle but not finding any answers.

Estelle grinned around the cigarette that was clamped between her lips. She blew a steady stream of smoke from the corner of her mouth and nodded.

"You're sharp, aren't you? And you say what you think. Reminds me of someone I used to know."

"Who?" Izzie was immediately curious. "Do they look like me?"

Estelle shook her head. "Not my story to tell. But I have a feeling you'll find out soon enough."

Izzie wanted to ask more questions, but Estelle raised her hand. "Not my story to tell. Don't keep after me like you didn't hear me."

Horace cleared his throat. "You girls should really not be out here tonight."

Alison ducked her chin. "We're pretty good at taking care of ourselves."

"Our walks remind us to not give in to the fear."

"Not to give in to the dark families. Our little protest."

Horace stirred the fire with an iron poker. "Don't repeat this, but I'm proud of you girls. But we still don't know how someone got on and off the campus. Twice, at least. I don't need to remind you what happened." He looked up at the girls, shaking his head. "Not one more."

"We're part of the solution; we have to be. This place belongs to us." Alison shook her fist. "Not going to let anyone take this from us without a fight."

"You," Estelle said to Alison. "You're different from the rest of the students. Drow magic. Not a lot of that left in this world."

"You've met a Drow before?"

"The questions could go on all night. I've already made myself clear."

Horace brushed the dirt off his hands. "I'll make you girls a deal because I know that telling you not to do something is not going to have any effect."

"We're listening."

"Something happens, anything at all, you come to find me and tell me. No questions asked, until maybe a lot later. Give me that so I can sleep at night, girls."

Alison could feel Izzie's questions swirling in her head. She bit her lip, forcing herself to focus. "Sounds reasonable. Fine, if we run into something, we'll tell you."

"This is where you head on back to the dorms." Estelle blew smoke rings in the direction of the cluster of buildings.

Alison pulled Izzie by the hand, even as Izzie opened her mouth to ask a question. Estelle smiled at her, waving goodbye.

When the girls were far enough away, Izzie started talking as fast as she could, the ideas spilling out of her.

"The people here are hiding the truth from me. I'm sure of it. She knew me! What does that mean? What kind of good reason could there be for not telling me everything she knows? And what was that about agreeing to run to Horace?"

Izzie bounced a few steps ahead of Alison, turned around and started walking backward, waving her arms, even as the questions kept coming.

"Whoa! Whoa, Izzie. That's a lot to process. I said we'd find them, but I didn't say how fast." Alison held up her hand. "I have no explanation for Estelle. What makes you so sure she has ever seen you before?"

"I don't know what it is. But I feel it here." She pressed a hand against her belly.

Alison hesitated before she grabbed Izzie's hand and dragged her back to the school. Once they were back in their room, Alison opened a drawer in her dresser and rummaged through it as quietly as she could. "Here it is," she whispered. She took out the book on counterspells that she had taken from the library.

"What are you doing?" Izzie whispered. "I know, I know, don't wake the others."

"I've been reading this book." Alison sat down on the edge of her bed, paging through it. "I found something I want to show you."

"What is it?" Izzie sat down next to Alison, flipping to a page with an illustration of an Oriceran beetle.

"Got it!" She pulled the book closer, even as Izzie leaned over to get a better look. "Still not sure what all the symbols mean. I can make out the words."

"I'm pretty sure this spell could finally remove whatever is blocking you."

Izzie's eyes widened as she stared at the page, her finger tracing the different symbols. "Let's do it, then. Right now." She grabbed Alison's hand, causing Alison to nearly drop the book.

Alison fumbled, stopping the book from falling loudly onto the ground and shook her head.

"We can't just *do* a spell. We don't know the full consequences. You remember what happened between you, me, and Tanner? We still don't know what that was all about. There are consequences to everything, and with magic, that could be anything."

"Then why are you showing it to me?" Izzie wasn't whispering anymore.

"Hold it down. I didn't say I wouldn't. Look, we need to get some more background first this time. I want to ask some of the others to help us. Tanner and Ethan, not to mention all our roommates. And you know Luke will be there as well." Alison put her arm around Izzie.

Izzie shook her head. "No, we are not asking them."

"Why not?"

"Because if this is dangerous like you said, I don't want to get anyone else into trouble or put them in danger. It's bad enough that something out there is hunting me."

"Might be me; we don't know for sure."

Kathleen rolled over in her sleep, lightly snoring.

"But this is a risk I'm willing to take for you. Trust me. I have an idea of how it feels not to know who you are—maybe not in the way that you feel it, but my life isn't exactly clean-cut, either."

"You have Shay and Brownstone. Family."

"I believe you. You have family out there, too. Besides, we have that bond, remember? I've been walking around in your head. I know how awful it is."

Izzie smirked, shrugging her shoulders. "Not all awful." She squeezed Alison's hand. "But I don't want anyone else involved."

"Fine, but at some point, we'll have to tell them." Alison grabbed Izzie's hand. "You're not alone. You've got all of us.

"Just for today, can we play this one my way? I can't take anyone getting hurt trying to help me."

The two girls smiled at each other in the dark. "Just for now."

"You're getting pretty good at this loophole thing. Okay, okay. Let's go. I really want to do this spell now." Izzie grabbed Alison's hand just as Kathleen let out a snort and smacked her lips.

They laughed, shushing each other as Izzie pulled her out of their dorm room.

"Where are we headed? Are we going back outside?"

"Technically, no."

Izzie led Alison down to the first floor, looking around before she opened the door to the supply closet.

"Wait, where are we? Not that I'm questioning your tactics."

"This is the School of Necessary Magic. Lots of things

around here are not as they seem." Izzie pulled in a small amount of energy and waved her arm in front of the back wall. It slowly faded, revealing a tunnel. "I found it one day when I was supposed to be getting some paper towels. Tripped over a bucket and a little flailing later, this appeared."

"And you never told me!"

"Only thing I've been keeping to myself. I was going to tell you, but then, dead girl, spooky dark magic professor, and bees everywhere. This seemed like a fun fact that could wait."

They crept down the tunnel, walking down stone steps that took them underground. Eventually, they came out on another side of the main building behind the stairs in an old coat closet.

"The old dude who donated this land must have had all of these built. Come on, the library is the perfect place. No one will be anywhere near it. The gnomes are either in bed or protecting the vault."

Alison closed the door with a click, and Izzie put the book on the table, paging through until she found the right spell again.

Together, the girls read through everything, muttering the words under their breath. "Do you know how to pronounce this one?"

"I think that word is *carmen*. Professor Hudson said that's common in spells that reveal truths. Shows up a lot in love spells too." Alison flipped through the book. "See, you see that word again and again."

"This could go wrong in a lot of different directions."

"Definitely."

"Let's do this. I have to know."

"Okay, now or never." Alison quietly pushed the table back against the wall. The two girls joined hands, letting the magic build inside of them and flow between the two.

Immediately, the atmosphere in the room changed, the particles in the air shifting to ice crystals. Alison and Izzie both shivered. "Still want to do this?"

Izzie could feel the air in the room pressing against her. The bond between them was thrown wide open. They stood looking at each other, not sure where one ended, and the other began.

"I have to know. I want to find my family." Izzie was breathing hard, her eyes glowing already.

They both closed their eyes, took a deep breath, and started chanting the memorized words from the book.

Cancellus de carmine cantatum menit, clauderus de carmen oblivisci fecit.

Their voices as one, the girls chanted the same words over and over again.

Cancellus de carmine cantatum menit, clauderus de carmen oblivisci fecit.

Cancellus de carmine cantatum menit, clauderus de carmen oblivisci fecit.

As they chanted, warmth grew where their palms touched each other. At first, it was only slight, but with every repetition, the heat grew until it was searing hot and almost unbearable. But their hands were fused together by the magic, and they could not let go of each other even if they'd wanted to. The air around them was still like ice. The contrast was jarring.

Alison felt the spell start draining her energy. Her legs

were trembling, and she felt as if her breath was being pushed out of her.

Izzie opened her eyes and looked at Alison, who was gritting her teeth. "You okay?" She was straining to say the words. But before Alison could reply, Izzie had a sudden, sharp headache that felt like someone had pushed a stake into her brain. She cried out, her back arching, and sharp pains shot into her temples. "It feels like someone is digging long, sharp nails into my brain."

"We need to stop!" Alison tried to pull her hand away.

Izzie squeezed her eyes shut, gritting her teeth, but just as she was ready to give up, the spell broke open.

The heat that was growing between them exploded, shooting Alison and Izzie away from each other. Alison crashed against a wall, knocking the wind out of her, and she slid to the floor. Izzie flew backward and took out three chairs before she came to a stop, half-draped over another chair. She pulled herself up on her elbows. Her eyes were open, but she was seeing everything from Alison's perspective. A world full of different colors. She put her hands out in front of her, feeling for the floor or a nearby wall. The only thing that was grounding her was her bond with Alison. She didn't have to be able to see to know that she was on the opposite side of the room from her friend.

Before Izzie could push off the chair and stand up, images hit her in quick succession, and she felt like she was being punched in the gut. Images of her parents—the faces of the man and woman she had seen in her dreams.

"Leira... Leira Berens. Mom," she whispered the name. "You're Mom." She watched her mother open a portal and leave for a distant destination. She pressed her back against the wall, still not seeing the room around her. "I've met you! You spoke here. She's a bounty hunter! Alison! Alison! Whoaaaa." There was her father. "Correk. That's my dad." Tears slid down her cheeks.

She put her arms out in the air, opening and shutting her hands.

On the other side of the room, Alison sat, dazed, listening to her friend and taking it all in.

"That's our home." Izzie saw their house in Washington, DC, her room upstairs, and her window facing the back-yard. Joy filled her, riding atop the magic. "I remember the way the light fell through the window in the mornings, how I used to curl up on the carpet and read a book on the weekends." She remembered her father singing her to sleep at night, and her mother waking her up by throwing open the curtains.

The memories kept on coming.

Dark wizards and witches who were hunting them. She saw the dark robes, and black magic chasing them. She remembered her parents fighting against them, sometimes allowing Izzie to jump in, but often shielding her away from it.

She pushed herself up against the wall, attempting to stand. "Alison, I remember! No, I remember the last… the last night." She struggled to get the words out. "I remember the last night we fought together. They made a deal!"

She shook her head, trying to regain her sight. Flashes of the room appeared then disappeared again. She could see Alison breathing hard across the room, absorbing the emotions running through Izzie.

"Dammit! They had no right! We were on the run, and we came here to see… to see…" She could feel her stomach churn. "Mara Berens… my great-grandmother."

Izzie cried out in pain. Her entire body ached as the spell that was cast over her three years ago released. Tears streamed down her cheeks. "She's been lying to me." Her words came out in a croak.

Izzie stood up without knowing what she was doing. The memories faded as the room came back in view.

Alison scrambled to her feet, tears streaming down her cheeks, too. "I can honestly say that I did not see that coming."

Through the bond that Izzie, Alison, and Tanner shared, Alison saw every image as it came to Izzie. She felt every memory, pain, or comfort that it brought. She felt how it threatened to rip her friend apart, even though it was the answer to every question. "Sometimes the answers can hurt like hell," she muttered.

Alison could feel in her muscles the hatred that flowed through Izzie's system.

"I'm going to find her and try out a few other spells." Izzie's stomach lurched as she tried to reach for the door. Her feet were unsteady underneath her.

"No, wait!" Alison jumped in front of Izzie before she could leave the library. "Don't do this, not yet."

"You can't stop me, Alison. Not this time. I have a bone to pick with my so-called great-grandmother."

She tried to push past Alison, but Alison braced herself with Drow energy.

"Just think about what you're doing. Look, something

about what you remembered is connecting some dots, but I can't quite put it together."

"I don't have to think about it," Izzie snapped. "You know how I feel, and you know what I saw. How can you tell me to stop?"

Alison shook her head. "No, you're not listening. Something is really nagging at me." She shook Izzie by the shoulders.

Despite Izzie's anger, she realized that there was something that Alison was trying to figure out. It calmed her rage enough to listen.

"Oh, my God, that's it," Alison gasped. She slapped her forehead. "The bees. It was in one of the books I was searching while Kathleen distracted the gnomes." Her excitement was building. "I came across the crest of one of the older dark families. Hang on, I have a piece of paper here somewhere."

She pulled out a piece of scrap paper and dug through her pocket for a pen. She quickly scribbled a picture of the crest, and at the top, she drew two bees. "Easy to miss with all the vines and deer antlers and weapons. A lot to look at." She spun the paper around to show Izzie. "That magical family was known for their ability to control the creatures around them. See? The bees, do you get it? It's a sign from the dark families. Lisa wasn't the end game. Her death was a vicious, cruel warning that we're just getting started. It was a throwdown!"

Izzie sucked in air, her heart rate jumping. "They're saying we're their puppets. They're declaring war, and we're on the frontlines."

"Exactly, we need to warn the headmistress, I mean… your great-grandmother. Wow, third generation."

"This is bad." Izzie's anger was starting to drain away.

"I think it's even a warning for the dark families who have kids here." Goose bumps ran over Alison's arms. The hair on the back of her neck stood up, sparking from the magic bristling near the surface.

"They're getting an early warning alert. That's why the bees have been popping up all semester. Notice how many families already left. They knew! They knew and said nothing to the rest of us." Izzie paced the room.

Alison nodded. "The ancient crest. The death. It's all happening again."

"Wait, what exactly was in that book?"

"It was about the last time this particular family was in power. There was a lot of death involved, in much larger numbers. This time, we appear to be their target."

"This is a lot to process. We have to get out of here and warn the others. Come on."

"Where are you going? Where are we going?" Alison ran after Izzie up the main stairs, not bothering to be quiet.

"Time is not on our side. We have to tell the others!" Izzie took the stairs two at a time.

Mara lay in her bed, drifting in and out of sleep. She opened her eyes and looked out the nearby window at the dark sky.

The conversation with the Mays had been terrible. She wasn't able to console them. When the Mays finally left, she had gone to her office and pulled out the small wooden box, looking inside at the three small orbs. They were almost completely dissolved. She carried it with her to her private quarters, stowing it in her closet.

She rolled on her back and looked at the ceiling. "Not much time left."

Boom!

The window panes rattled, the sound coming from her closet.

The box. She jumped out of bed and ran to the closet. The wooden box was a pile of ashes.

"No, no, no…" Mara picked up the ashes and watched as the dust fell through her fingers.

The spell was broken.

In a daze, she swung the safe shut, locking the ashes in as if it would make a difference. She sat down on the floor of her closet.

"Bitch, I know you're my great-grandmother." Izzie Berens stood in the doorway of her bedroom with her hands on her hips. Alison was close behind her. "And we're going to talk about every bit of that, but right now, we've got news. The dark families are coming to take us down, and soon."

CHAPTER TWENTY

Jason Parker crept out of the boys' dorm in the middle of the night, wearing a school hoodie.

A shiver ran down his spine, and he swallowed hard, trying to convince himself that what he was doing was the right thing. It was what he was here for, after all. He pulled out his phone and looked at all the missed calls from his father. "Do it or be disinherited," he muttered. "I get it. I get it." He shoved the phone back in his pocket. "I am in too deep. Gotta finish it."

A wave of magic rocked his body at the front door, and he froze. His phone buzzed again, and his dad's face appeared on the screen. "No, no." He shook his head. "In too deep."

Jason turned back and went down the hallways to his locker. He opened it and retrieved the device he had stolen from the Young Entrepreneurs class.

He closed his locker and let himself out the front door. This was it. It was time.

Jason made his way across the circular driveway, trying his best not to think about Lisa's body maimed by bee stings. "I am so sorry," he said to the open space.

It was the night of a new moon, and there was hardly any light. It meant that Jason would not easily be spotted, and he was glad. After all this time at the school, working his way into the minds of some of the students and secretly putting the systems in place, he did not want to be found out now.

He reached the front gates, the Oriceran symbol visible despite the darkness. He lifted the device and activated it. It started humming and trembling, the parts rattling. "Yes, it's working."

It deactivated the wards and was breaking the spell on the gates.

He clutched the device with one hand, struggling not to drop it, and with the other hand, he pulled the heavy gate open. Despite the help of the device, the gate was still almost impossible to move. It felt as if the steady stream of magic held it shut. Still, Jason managed to crack the gate open just wide enough.

He grunted, bracing himself with his knees bent, and his feet digging into the gravel as he fought to keep the gate open, and the device active.

One by one, dark wizards and witches came out of the nearby darkness and slipped through the opening in the gate. They were wearing black robes. Their hoods were pulled over their heads to hide their faces.

"Hello, hi, hello." He nodded at each of them, as they ignored him or scowled.

He was struggling with the device to keep the gates open and not set off the alarms.

The witches and wizards were here for a battle. The end was finally here.

The wizards and witches moved as if they floated, the robes fluttering in the breeze like a real-life version of the Grim Reaper.

They spread out in a half-moon and moved toward the school in a staggered line that could not be stopped.

Mara was about to answer Izzie when darkness flooded the room.

Izzie reached out to grab Alison. "Is this part of the spell?"

"I don't think so. This is coming from something else. Someplace dark."

"Something is very, very wrong." Mara looked out the window at the school grounds. She sent out a small ball of light, zipping toward the front gate and saw the reflection.

"The gates are open!" She opened the window and leaned out, watching the reflection from the light she sent. "Two moons," she gasped. "Look!" She could see the army of dark wizards and witches flooding onto the school grounds one by one.

Mara closed her eyes, pushing back against the fear that clawed at her, and dug deep for the strongest magic she knew. She pushed all the fear away and focused her energy on her core.

"Absoluta exitium." She threw her arms wide. The Level

One warning traveled across the grounds. It raced across the ground, whispering to everyone it ran into, breaking in every direction, and raising the whispers to a roar.

The school is under attack. Man your stations.

She could feel the tremble in the ground beneath the school. It was like the magic beneath her feet answered, sending a message back. Next, the spell made its way to the kemana beneath the school, and to magicals living there, notifying them of the danger.

The end is near. Send help.

Mara wasn't going to wait for anyone to appear. She turned and bolted from the room. She was going to face this terrible evil, while her forces gathered.

Her warning spell woke every student and professor on the property. They spilled out of their rooms, running for the dining hall—the prearranged gathering place—and overflowed into the hallway. Even the kitchen pixies were already there, holding ladles and rolling pins over their heads.

Mara stood on the stairs by the dining room and sent up a spray of sparks to draw everyone's attention.

"Quiet! There's very little time. Only minutes. Until now, you have been students in my school learning how to use new magic. And tonight, you will use all of that to defend our school. Our grounds have been infiltrated by an army of dark wizards and witches. They're coming."

A ripple of fear ran through the students, and they all started talking.

"Get your wands, pull in your energy, draw on whatever you have to fight back! There is no time to move all of you. I know you can do it. You are all better than you think you are. I have watched you grow and learn, and I am proud of every one of you. Do what you can and pick your battles carefully. Team up, so you're never alone. We have to face these people and stop them. And we are not the only ones fighting—I have sent for help."

There wasn't time to give the students more of a pep talk. The professors were already creating smaller groups of the students, taking off with them to scout the grounds.

"For the school!" A student bellowed, followed by a loud cheer.

They poured out of the school, running into the wizards and witches just behind the circular driveway. They had formed a kind of front line, a wall of black robes and dark magic. Immediately, the first spells were hurled, streaks of dark magic seeking out a target.

Mara's eyes glowed in the dark. The symbols on her arms glowed and spread up her neck. Set an intention. She called into the dark to all the women in her line, summoning their magic. Eireka Berens, Leira Berens, and even Izzie Berens blending their power together. Eireka answered immediately, her magic joining her mother's, sending a blast of power at the first witch in front of her. The battle was underway.

Aya and Emma jumped in, raising their wands and giving each other confidence. Kathleen and Ethan threw fireballs in opposite directions, circling some of the dark wizards. Others were summoning magic, mumbling spells, and teaming up just as Mara had commanded. In groups of two or three, the students took on each dark witch or wizard.

"Bring it, bitches!" Scarlett let out a war whoop, shooting out fireballs in rapid fire.

"We're not going to be able to pull this off alone," said Tanner, catching up to Alison and Izzie. "Where the hell have you two been? Whatever you were doing, what a rush!"

"Finding out the truth." Izzie saw the bracelet rattling on her wrist and pushed it up her arm. She felt the internal tug from her grandmother's magic and was about to ignore her when the magical nudge arrived from her mother, Leira Berens.

Leira's Jasper energy was joining the fight from afar. She felt the familiar buzzing warmth of her mother's magic, at last. "Mom." Her eyes shone with tears. "We will be together again."

"We're not alone! Look!" Peter pointed toward the back of the school grounds. Magicals from the kemana were flooding out of the woods. The kemana's glow could be seen all the way to the front.

"That is some badass magic," whispered Alison.

Wood elves, Light Elves, witches, wizards, and fairies. Willens and Kilomeas were running into the fray side by side. Every creature was emptying out of the kemana. Mara's warning spell had gone far and wide down every street of the underground city, and magicals were swarming the grounds.

"There's hope," whispered Kathleen.

The magicals charged the dark witches and wizards, flanking them on the sides in an intense clash of light and dark. Wood elves shifted their scales, blending into the dark landscape, their pupils scanning in different directions. They attacked with the element of surprise on their side. A witch screamed as a wood elf jumped on her and set her afire. She tried to get out a dark spell, but it was difficult to concentrate when the magical inflicted so much pain.

Two fairies were holding back a wizard's arms and flapping their silver wings. They flew up with the wizard until they were so high that a fall would mean certain death. They looked at each other, nodded, and let go.

"Don't mess with a faerie." Alison pushed a wall of Drow magic, knocking over a row of witches.

The sound of the wizard's scream as he fell to his death was muffled by the sound of fighting.

Even the dragon, Dorvu was involved. He flew over the wizards and witches blowing a continuous wave of ice over them. He froze some of them where they stood, and some of them slipped on the ice formed on the driveway causing their magic to bounce out of control.

Mara's energy built up inside of her, nearly burning her. She blasted a wizard standing in front of her. He managed to deflect her magic, turning the magic back on her.

The headmistress twisted her hands, working a spell to redirect the blast, but it wasn't working fast enough. She braced for the impact.

Just as the piercing fire was about to ignite her, Xander Powell stepped in front and deflected the magic with ease.

He looked over his shoulder when the danger was averted. "Are you okay?"

Mara nodded, stunned. "You came to my rescue." It brought back a flood of memories from long ago.

"Better shake it, girl. I'm good, but I can't fight all of them alone." Xander smiled at her, waving his wand and hurling a wizard hard against a tree.

The professors were using their areas of expertise as they fought the witches and wizards. Professor Fowler used potions she'd turned into mists or gasses to burn the witches and wizards, attacking with spells once they were immobilized. She managed to blind three wizards, putting them out of commission with a potion.

Professor Regency took all the magic that danced around him—the remnants of spells cast by the students—and channeled it, throwing sharp hooks at the witch, who was screaming chants, coming at him. The magical hooks hit her, her scream changing from rage to terror as she tried to counter it. But it was too little too late, and the magic pierced her chest, striking her down.

Two students took over, attacking the next adversaries with what they had learned last semester.

Professor Regency moved down the battle line to face off against more wizards, confident the students were capable of taking over and not getting injured or worse, killed.

Together, the magicals fought the darkness infiltrating the grounds, but somehow, it wasn't enough. Even though they were winning a lot of the battles, Mara feared they were losing the war. The magic they were fighting was very old and layered, clinging to its victims.

Alison used her Drow energy, and martial arts she'd

learned from Shay, holding up a shield made of shadow that she conjured out of thin air. The magic reached her, bouncing off the shield and sending thin cracks throughout it, but it held.

Izzie caught a spell meant to dry her flesh and drain her of any blood, rolled it up with her Jasper magic, and threw it right back at the witch who easily countered it.

"You think you're so clever," the witch sneered. "Do you think I don't know how to block my own magic?"

"Fair enough." Alison joined her, kicking the witch in the face with a back kick that sent her spiraling to the ground. She hit the earth with a loud thud. "We were just distracting you."

The witch cackled and jumped up again. "Touché," she said. "But this is far from over."

"Good," Izzie said. "We were just getting warmed up, and now that I know who I am, bitch, you're in trouble."

Izzie threw lines of magic at the witch that burned stripes on her arms, crept up her body, and wrapped her tightly in a blue flame that wouldn't extinguish. The witch screamed and tried to swat out the fire that ate her black robe. Her hood fell back, and Izzie could see her face. If she weren't a dark being, she might have been pretty.

When the witch managed to kill the flames, she looked at Izzie with wide eyes, her face tortured from the pain.

"Are you—?" she cried, pointing her finger.

Alison saw the witch open her mouth to spread the word. They had found Leira Berens' child.

"Enough trouble."

Anger flooded Alison, unlocking her Drow magic. She felt it growing inside, every molecule trembling with the magic. She threw her hands toward the witch, and her magic flew toward the dark being in a stream of shadows and darkness. It wrapped around the witch like ribbon and started squeezing. The witch screamed as she tried to get free of the constraints that Alison's magic placed on her, but she could do nothing to get out of it.

"I have had just about enough of you coming into our school and hurting my friends," Alison shouted. The witch strained to lift her wand and created a spell aimed at Izzie, a death blow.

Izzie started to gag, grabbing at her throat, and immediately turned blue.

"No!" Alison felt the fear in her chest of losing her best friend. She squeezed her hands into fists, and the ribbon of shadows and darkness around the witch did the same, snapping her neck. The witch fell to the ground, limp.

"Oh, my God, she's dead. You saved my life." Izzie gulped in air as she looked at the body on the ground.

"No one fucks with my friend," Alison growled. She had never been this angry, and it activated her magic in a way that was addictive.

Tanner, Ethan, and Peter fought together on the other side of the school. A wizard had managed to get them away from the larger group, but the three of them were still standing together. He threw steady streams of dark magic at them, and the three boys managed to counter it just the way they had learned from Professor Powell.

A stream of magic got through their defense, hitting Peter in the center of his chest. Even though Peter hadn't been in the infirmary in a while, the dark magic still lingered in his system. The moment the black magic touched his chest, he cried out and fell to the ground. His old injuries ripped at his body, causing immense pain to flow through him. Tears squeezed out of his eyes, and he couldn't breathe.

Tanner fell to his knees to check on him. The wizard threw another dark spell at them, but Ethan managed to deflect it. He screamed a spell at the wizard, and when the magic pushed the darkness away, he was just as surprised as the wizard was.

Ethan looked at his hands. "I'm having an unusually good day at this."

"Timing is everything, dude."

The dark magic was averted, but all that power still had to go somewhere, and it flew toward the main building. With a loud crash, it broke through the wall of the dining hall, leaving a gaping hole in its wake as bricks crumbled and fell.

"Oh, shit," Ethan said. "Made another entrance to the dining hall!"

"It happens. Keep going." Tanner kept moving his wand, getting back to his feet, the lights flashing around his face.

The wizard didn't waste time. He used the distraction by the damage and ran.

"Oh, no you don't," Luke said. He shifted into wolf form and howled, calling to his pack, and took off after the wizard.

The stench of the dark wizard was in his nose, and magic ruffled his fur as his paws hit the ground in quick succession. He threw his head back and howled, a sound that was designed to instill fear.

The wizard ran, his arms churning. He glanced over his shoulder, lifting his trembling wand.

Luke caught up to the wizard with ease and jumped on his back, shoving him to the ground. Luke opened his jaws and clamped his fangs into the wizard's neck, shaking his head back and forth until the wizard was dead. He bit the wand into pieces, scattering it to the wind and dragged the wizard under some bushes.

That's for Peter.

He turned and trotted back to where Peter lay on the ground. Ethan and Tanner were both tending to him.

"Is he okay?" Luke asked after he shifted back into human form.

"I don't know. But I think he will be."

The students and professors fought hard. The magicals from the kemana chased the dark witches and wizards into the recesses of the school, battling from one hallway to the next. A Kilomea threw them one at a time out of a third-floor window, while more than one willen was able to separate a witch from her wand. But still, they were losing ground. Students were being injured left and right. The professors couldn't focus on the battle and instead turned their attention to saving the kids. The magicals, as brave as they were, were either getting hurt or worse, killed.

A scream rose behind the wizards, and Drow magic swirled around them, crushing against them.

"Don't you get the bigger picture?" Alison's magic was surging, causing her voice to echo. "This is our school and our people. We are not going to let you crush us or the world that we love."

The wizards only laughed, shaking their heads and turning toward Alison.

"What you don't get, little girl, is that this world is no longer yours."

Anger coursed through Alison in quantities she had never experienced before. She reached down deep inside to the magic she'd inherited from her mother. She remembered the day she lost her mother, the tragedy that had struck her down and had threatened to take her out. She remembered her father, the asshole who had set up her mother so that she had died. She remembered the pain when she had found out her father had betrayed them, and the horror of knowing that she was an orphan.

At the school, Alison had found people that she called family, and she had found magic inside her that rooted her in who she was even more than ever before. She was not about to let that go.

"Graaaaaagh!"

Her power grew until the wizards could feel it, and they knew they were in trouble. They raised their wands in unison, ready to crush the teenage girl, but Alison was done playing nice. She grabbed her magic into her hands and slammed it down, smashing the wizards until all that was left of them were puffs of black dust.

Mara blinked, stunned by Alison's power. "I'm going to have to help that girl control her power. How is this even possible?"

Alison spun around and was ready to do the same to anyone else who dared to keep coming. But the others had stopped fighting. Instead, they'd turned and were running.

"Yeah, run," Alison shouted after them. "Tell everyone!

If you come back, I'll finish the job. I am Alison Brown-stone, Drow Princess, student of this school, and future bounty hunter."

The witches and wizards were gone, and the silence over the grounds was so strong that it made everyone stand still, listening for the slightest sound. There was nothing.

Everyone turned and stared at Alison, who was slowly gaining control over her anger.

Izzie ran to Alison and grabbed her into a hug. "I can't believe you just did that!"

The full effect of the battle hit her. "Neither can I."

"I don't think any of us can." Mara walked toward the girls.

Izzie spun around, glaring at Mara. "You betrayed me."

"Izzie, choose between forgiveness or bitterness. You have to do it now. Either one is going to take root. What is it you want?"

Izzie narrowed her eyes. She could still feel the strength of all the women in her line answering the call to lend their magic. "I choose forgiveness, but when this is all done, I'm still going to need an explanation."

"Great-granddaughter." Mara opened her arms wide, reaching for Izzie. She felt the weight of the last three years of loneliness.

"Izzie…go." Alison pushed her best friend in the small of her back toward her great-grandmother. Izzie fell into her arms, pressing her face into her shoulder. "Nana, Nana."

"What now?"

Sparks appeared in the driveway, and some of the students jumped back. Others prepared themselves for yet another fight.

A portal opened, and a stunned Leira and Correk stepped onto the school grounds. Behind them, Yumfuck jumped out and scrambled up to Correk's shoulder.

They looked around, taking in the damage, the injured and tired students, and the bodies of the few magicals who didn't make it.

Yumfuck immediately jumped off Correk's shoulder, growing to his full eight feet, his body bulging and stretching until the troll was terrifying, and he let out a roar that made the ground tremble.

Some of the teenagers cringed, wondering what to do next. But Mara smiled, hugging her great-granddaughter tighter.

"Down, big guy." Mara held out her hand to him. "The bad guys have already fled the scene."

"I missed the fun?" The troll shrunk down to five inches, waving to the crowd. "Aloha, motherfuckers!"

"What the fuck happened here?" Leira looked at the gaping hole in the dining hall. "I don't know if Turner Underwood will like your renovations, but it could work."

"It's a very long and familiar story," Mara said with a sigh.

"The dark families... I hope you finally crushed them."

"Drow magic may have finally done it."

"Mom! Dad!" Izzie yelled, running to her parents.

"Oh, my child!" Leira spun around in time to catch

Izzie, who had lunged into her mother's arms. "I'm so glad you're safe."

"I remember everything!"

"Look how much you've grown." Correk wrapped his arms around his two girls. "The three of us are united at last."

Leira looked over Izzie's shoulder as she held her daughter and noticed Alison standing a few feet away, digging her toe in the dirt.

"Thank you."

Alison looked confused. "For what?"

Leira gave her a crooked smile. "Such humility. For saving Izzie's life."

Alison smiled and nodded. "She is a very special person and my best friend."

"Absolutely," Correk said.

"I have to go see to the injured. We'll talk soon. You can catch up in my quarters, what's left of them." Mara helped what was left of her staff round up the students and get them to the safest shelter while some helped the nurse rush the injured to the still standing infirmary.

"Mara, tend to your family. You've waited long enough for this moment." Eleanor Hudson had a welt across her forehead. She touched it gingerly. "Don't worry about this. The other guy looks a lot worse and a little dead. Go to your family and take all of them."

"You mean Xander Powell."

"He's the girl's great-grandfather. Speak of the devil."

Xander Powell cautiously approached them.

"He's part of their side!" Izzie's eyes grew wide, and she pulled in energy, her eyes glowing.

"No, wait!" Mara stepped between them. "Some of this is my doing. He's not the enemy, not now anyway." She let out a deep sigh. "This is not easy. Izzie, this is your great-grandfather." Mara looked at Leira as she said the words.

"What the hell? My long, lost grandfather? Nana, you can keep a secret better than anyone I know." Leira held out her hand for the troll as he jumped over from Correk's shoulder.

"I'm afraid we can't have a long reunion," said Correk, looking Xander up and down.

"Wondering about our taste in men in this family?" Leira arched an eyebrow, smiling.

"Not exactly consistent."

"Good save."

"What will you do now? There are still forces out there trying to kill you. And now your cover and who your daughter is, it's all out in the open again." Mara scowled at the gaping hole in the building.

"It doesn't matter what we do, Mara. Now, we're going to do it as a family."

Correk nodded. "Izzie is much older, now. She can fend for herself a lot more easily. We'll be okay."

"Let's at least take this inside."

CHAPTER TWENTY-ONE

I n the weeks that followed, the school quickly returned
to its normal routines. The kitchen pixies helped by
organizing the magicals from the kemana to fix the
damage to the old manor.

"The first thing *we're* going to work on is the dining hall
and kitchen." Professor Hudson clapped her hands, glad to
have something to do. "After that, we start on the classrooms. Don't want you missing any school. No groaning,
please. Chop, chop!"

Classes resumed after only a day's break. The Louper
match was rescheduled, and some of the students who had
left the school after Lisa's disappearance called about
coming back again. No one from the dark families made an
inquiry.

And for the first time in years, Mara was able to sleep
well despite still missing one student, Jason Parker. They
had searched for him everywhere, and his distraught father

threatened a lawsuit and darker measures until they showed him the proof of what Jason had done.

"But then, you already knew that didn't you," Mara had said, keeping her voice even and calm.

The students ate lunch in the dining hall. A spell kept the wind from blowing through the gaping hole.

Eleanor Hudson walked up to Mara where she was standing on the small stage, looking out over the tables.

"The chaos has been curbed." Professor Hudson folded her hands in front of her, her wand neatly tucked in her pocket.

"It seems so," Mara said with a sigh. "I'm still not used to the absence of dread."

"You did good, Mara. You helped us all to save the school."

Mara smiled and looked at the professor. "Thank you," she said. "That means more than you know. I'm going to rename the dining hall. I'm going to name this the Lisa May Hall."

Hudson looked out over the students again and nodded.

"I think that's the right way to go about it."

Izzie sat with her parents at one of the tables. Alison was right next to her, with the rest of their friends.

Under the table, Leira held Izzie's hand. She leaned against Correk's shoulder. "I got a second chance I didn't even remember I needed."

Alison nudged Izzie, and they laughed watching Estelle

in the kitchen, sitting on a stool, smoking her cigarette and telling the pixies long stories.

Estelle saw the girls watching and hopped off the stool, casually sucking on her cigarette and blowing a circle into the air. Estelle seemed relieved when she stepped through the hole and into the dining room. She walked toward the table, cigarette clamped between her lips, and planted her hands on her hips.

"It's about time we had a family reunion," she said.

Correk laughed. "Estelle, you're practically beaming."

Estelle shrugged, patting her tall bouffant. "You can sweet-talk me all you want, Correk, but that doesn't mean you're off the hook. There is a lot that needs to be done, and you better get cracking." She turned around and marched back to the kitchen. The pixies all cheered as she stepped back into the kitchen.

Leira laughed as Estelle walked away.

Horace came into the dining room and strolled toward their table just after Estelle left. He glanced toward the kitchen where he saw his aunt entertaining the pixies and chuckled.

"I see my aunt is helping out."

"The pixies just love her."

Horace laughed. "Well, they're going to have to get used to it. We all are. Estelle has decided to stay for a little while and help the school rebuild."

"You know what I'm looking forward to?" Luke asked. "The next Louper tournament. Once we get to do that, I feel like everything will be back to normal."

The teenagers started talking about the next tournament.

Mara arrived at the table, and the conversation died down again.

"Are you talking about the Louper tournament?" she asked.

The students all nodded.

"About that…"

The atmosphere suddenly became tense. The students looked at each other. Luke looked worried—what if the tournament was canceled?

"I think it's exactly what we need, no matter the winner."

CHAPTER TWENTY-TWO

The Great Hall was decorated in twinkling lights everywhere. Eleanor noticed Xander on the other side of the room, talking to another professor.

"Why don't you go talk to him?" Eleanor noticed that Mara was looking, too.

Mara shook her head. "I don't think so. I don't have anything to say to him."

Eleanor nodded. "You have a lifetime of things to talk about." She gave Mara a pointed look.

Mara sighed and nodded. "I'm only going because I can't stand to walk away from everything."

"I know, I use it against you on a regular basis."

Mara approached Xander cautiously. He waved away the other professor and crossed his arms, waiting. "Well?"

"Eleanor seems to think we'll be able to fix the final damage," Mara said, making small talk.

"Nothing a little bit of magic can't fix. You came over here to give me a magical construction update?"

"Look, Xander, I am sorry. For all of it. For hiding Izzie's real identity from you."

Xander shrugged. "You already apologized."

"I know. But that doesn't change that I feel awful about it."

"It's not that I don't accept your apology, Mara," Xander said tightly, "but it will take time."

"Well, we have some of that, right?"

His face softened. "Yes, I guess we do."

Luke hugged Izzie tightly around the neck. "This is not over. We'll find a way to see each other again."

"If magic exists in the world…"

"Then anything is possible."

"I'll find you, one way or another."

Luke hugged her again and whispered into her ear. "Someday, I will hold you again." He let go and turned around, walking away before anyone could see the tears in his eyes.

Alison saw the pain in his soul and stepped forward. She knew how he felt. "When will I see you again?" Alison gave Izzie a locket with their pictures in it. "Easy to take on the run with you."

Izzie smiled. "I'll find a way to stay in touch and let you know how we're doing. We have to do this."

Alison nodded. "I get it, and I'm going to believe that one day we'll get to take walks late at night together again."

"One day, I promise. Keep an eye open for my messages. I'll make sure to find a way."

"It's not just that," Alison said. "I just want you to be safe."

Izzie nodded. "I will be. Some of that spell we did with Tanner is still in us. You'll always know that I'm somewhere safe."

Alison hugged Izzie, squeezing tightly, not wanting to let her friend go.

Leira came to the girls.

"Are you ready?" she asked Izzie, who nodded. "Alison, I want to thank you again. Not only for saving Izzie but for being a friend to my daughter when she had nothing in this world. It means so much to me. And I know it means everything to her."

Izzie nodded, and Alison felt close to tears.

"And from what I've heard," Leira continued, "you have the makings of greatness in you. You are going to be one badass bounty hunter. You could change things, help it evolve, and solve the crimes. Not just catch the bad guys."

Alison blushed and smiled. Maybe Leira was right. Hearing those words from the original bounty hunter was an enormous compliment.

All too soon, it was time for Izzie to go. She hugged Alison one more time, and Alison held on for as long as she could.

"We are badass." Izzie gave a crooked smile as Alison laughed, looking back and forth between mother and daughter.

"Don't know why I didn't see that before." She hugged Izzie one last time.

Correk opened a portal in the dining room, and Leira,

Izzie, and Yumfuck stepped through. He stepped through last, holding the opening for as long as he could.

Everyone shouted their goodbyes as the family disappeared, sparks hitting the floor

Alison watched as the portal closed, the final sparks shooting into the area before they fizzled and died out. She took a deep breath and chewed on her bottom lip. Aya, Kathleen, and Emma came up and put their arms around her. Peter, Ethan, Tanner and Luke came over and stood nearby. "She'll be back some day. Until then, you have us," said Kathleen.

"I'll miss her, but I learned something in that battle. We can make our own future, especially when we work together. We can make sure the School of Necessary Magic comes back better than ever for our senior year."

"We are a force to be reckoned with," shouted Aya.

With a Drow Princess as the new leader of the pack.

The End

Life, and school, is hard without your best friend. Alison returns for her senior year, but someone is missing from her side.

And dark magic isn't done with her or her friends.

Alison returns for another adventure at the School of Necessary Magic in Determined is Her Path.

What's funnier than a swearing, troublemaking troll?

A trick or treating swearing, troublemaking troll.

Sign-up and keep up to date with all things Oriceran and receive a free copy of Trick or Troll, a short story starring YTT. (Other people are in it, too.)

GET IT NOW!

I'm sitting in the Orlando airport near the rental car counter waiting for one of my sisters to arrive so we can drive to a hospital about an hour away. My oldest sister is failing – best way to put it – and we are going to gather in the same room for the first time in six years. Since my mother's funeral. Family is complicated – there's a lot packed into those three words, but you get it.

Meanwhile, this week one friend's dad had a heart attack and another's ex who lives down the block suddenly died, leaving a young daughter without a dad. It's been a weird week, and I've been oddly peaceful. Ever since that day in October nine years ago that I was told I was terminal with a year left, my thinking has changed on all of it. The events I judge as good, the ones I have to journey through to get to the other side are no longer seen as harbingers, omens or signs of anything. None of it lasts forever, it's all part of the journey.

That means, I no longer stare at any one particular

event and let it loom large over the rest of my life, letting it all roll over, again and again, replaying each bit of the event, analyzing it from every angle. I'm tired just reciting that old list.

I call that old habit, catastrophizing. Step 2 – I do my best not to attached words like good or bad. That's my judgment on the events and when I can manage to cut it out, I tend to not only see the small and wonderful moments, the rest of it doesn't manage to root so deeply in my emotional memory. Step 3 – I no longer insist everyone do their best to feel happy all the time. I shake my head at the memories and how many times that was exactly what I wanted out of everyone. I know I saw negative emotions as dangerous – a portend of bad things. Maybe if we all join hands and smile then things will be okay.

Kind of obnoxious, now that I look back at it. Instead, I'm out here letting people feel what they want to feel – it's not a sign of anything other than how they feel. Revolutionary. My own drama-o-meter then stays pretty calm.

Step 4 – I welcome in my own emotions – all of them – anger, joy, sadness, celebration. Whatever they are, I let them be and wonder what message there is inside of it all. No more fear of what it could all mean. Maybe they're here to teach me something that I need to learn. It's that trust thing. Apparently, mine has been growing. (It was probably Yumfuck, he's taught me a lot)

So, here I sit in the airport, waiting without expectation, ready to continue on the next part of the journey, whatever it holds. More adventures to follow.

PS Michael will probably *never* read this far... Next

year, I'll finally be releasing the urban fantasy series, The Peabrain Adventures (he's not fond of that title – I lurv it – that's a *Southern* word) and it's on. We have a friendly wager going that if the series is successful, he's more than happy to congratulate me from a podium. My assistant, Felicia the wonderful and I are having a blast mapping out our strategy. So, stick with us, stay tuned and if you see Anderle, tell him the Peabrain army is building…

First, THANK YOU for not only reading this book but these *Author Notes* as well.

This set of stories is aimed at a younger set of readers. (Mind you, I realize at times the language might suggest otherwise, but I digress.)

Right now, I am sitting just on the other side of fifty years old, not feeling all that different than when I was forty or thirty, or even twenty at some level.

The difference is experience allowing me the chance to see more outcomes that can occur than what the fear in my mind suggests will happen.

When I was a teenager, I wanted to be special, unique; someone others talked about (in a good way. I learned I could easily be talked about in bad ways, no problem) because of my talents or accomplishments.

For most of my life, none of that came true. I grew older, acquired skills by hard work or paying others to teach me, got married and had kids, etc., etc.. I reined in my desire to be special and learned how to be happy with being special to a select few people.

Instead of becoming a rock superstar (yes, I admit it), I became a person a handful of individuals liked to talk to day in and day out. Week after week we enjoyed playing video games, watching movies as our kids grew up.

My success as a best-selling author was not only unexpected at forty-eight, it wasn't even a fantasy I thought about anymore.

But that didn't mitigate the desire to be special which had lain dormant for decades.

In 2016, I had to fight my ego as my success grew. Even as an "almost" fifty-year-old, the desires of our youth are often ready to make themselves known as we strive to accomplish our goals. Fortunately, I was mature enough to deal (to the best of my ability) with the downsides of success with a stubbornness to work on handling it with humility (not always my strength, I'll admit.)

Right now, I'm sitting in the eating area of a Hampton Inn in New York, just a few minutes from JFK Airport. I'm on my way to Texas from Frankfurt, Germany and the book fair which just took place. I was able to enjoy eating and speaking with fans who knew nothing about me three years ago (because my first book, *Death Becomes Her*, wasn't released for a few more weeks.)

Just three short years later, thirty years of desire to be someone connected with thirty years of skills learned from other jobs and other ventures and exploded into what has become LMBPN. Around the world, fans read our stories, authors collaborate, and others work to produce new content every single day.

Whether you are fifteen years old as you read this author note or fifty-five, you never know when your dreams will come true and take you by surprise.

You have blessed this "older" man by reading one of our stories. Thank you, wherever you are on this planet we call Earth, for supporting us.

May you uncover your own dreams in your life, no matter how old you are.

Ad Aeternitatem,

Michael Anderle

OTHER REVELATION OF ORICERAN
UNIVERSE BOOKS

The Unbelievable Mr. Brownstone

* Michael Anderle *

Feared by Hell (1) - Rejected by Heaven (2) - Eye For An Eye (3) - Bring the Pain (4) - She is the Widow Maker (5) - When Angels Cry (6) - Fire with Fire (7) - Hail To The King (8) - Alison Brownstone (9) - One Bad Decision (10) - Fatal Mistake (11) - Karma Is A Bitch (12)

I Fear No Evil

* Martha Carr and Michael Anderle *

Kill the Willing (1) - Bury the Past, But Shoot it First (2) - Reload Faster (3) - Dead In Plain sight (4) - Tomb Raiding PHD (5) - Tomb Raider Emeritus (6)

School of Necessary Magic

* Judith Berens *

Dark Is Her Nature (1) Bright Is Her Sight (2) - Wary Is Her Love (3) - Strong Is Her Hope (4) - Wicked Is Her Smile (5) - Strange Is Her Life (6)

Rewriting Justice

* Martha Carr and Michael Anderle *

Justice Served Cold (1) - Vengeance Served Hot (2) - Bounty Hunter Inc (03) - Beware The Hunter (4)

The Leira Chronicles

* Martha Carr and Michael Anderle *

Waking Magic (1) - Release of Magic (2) - Protection of Magic (3)
- Rule of Magic (4) - Dealing in Magic (5) - Theft of Magic (6) -
Enemies of Magic (7) - Guardians of Magic (8)

The Soul Stone Mage Series

* Sarah Noffke and Martha Carr *

House of Enchanted (1) - The Dark Forest (2) - Mountain of
Truth (3) - Land of Terran (4) - New Egypt (5) - Lancothy (6) -
Virgo (7)

The Kacy Chronicles

* A.L. Knorr and Martha Carr *

Descendant (1) - Ascendant (2) - Combatant (3) - Transcendent
(4)

The Midwest Magic Chronicles

* Flint Maxwell and Martha Carr*

The Midwest Witch (1) - The Midwest Wanderer (2) - The
Midwest Whisperer (3) - The Midwest War (4)

The Fairhaven Chronicles

* with S.M. Boyce *

Glow (1) - Shimmer (2) - Ember (3) - Nightfall (4)

BOOKS BY MICHAEL ANDERLE

For a complete list of books by Michael Anderle, please visit

www.lmbpn.com/ma-books/

All LMBPN Audiobooks are Available at Audible.com and
iTunes. For a complete list of audiobooks visit:

www.lmbpn.com/audible

CONNECT WITH THE AUTHORS

Martha Carr Social

Website: http://www.marthacarr.com

Facebook:
https://www.facebook.com/groups/MarthaCarrFans/

Michael Anderle Social

Website: http://kurtherianbooks.com/

Email List: http://kurtherianbooks.com/email-list/

Facebook Here:
https://www.facebook.com/TheKurtherianGambitBooks/

www.ingramcontent.com/pod-product-compliance
Lightning Source LLC
Chambersburg PA
CBHW050234110726
47898CB00007B/2149